5.2

P9-DGB-326

sang
spell

PHYLLIS REYNOLDS NAYLOR

sang

spell

A JEAN KARL BOOK

ALADDIN PAPERBACKS

New York   London   Toronto   Sydney   Singapore

If you purchased this book without a cover you should be aware that this book is stolen property. It was reported as "unsold and destroyed" to the publisher and neither the author nor the publisher has received any payment for this "stripped book."

First Aladdin Paperbacks edition April 2000

Text copyright © 1998 by Phyllis Reynolds Naylor

Aladdin Paperbacks
An imprint of Simon & Schuster
Children's Publishing Division
1230 Avenue of the Americas
New York, NY 10020

All rights reserved, including the right of reproduction in whole or in part in any form.

Also available in an Atheneum Books for
Young Readers hardcover edition.
Designed by Angela Carlino
The text for this book was set in Dutch 766 BT.
Printed and bound in the United States of America
2 4 6 8 10 9 7 5 3 1

The Library of Congress has cataloged the
hardcover edition as follows:
Naylor, Phyllis Reynolds.
Sang Spell / Phyllis Reynolds Naylor.-1st ed.
p. cm.
"A Jean Karl book."
Summary: When his mother is killed in an automobile accident,
high-schooler Josh decides to hitchhike across the country,
and finds himself trapped in a mysterious village somewhere
in the Appalachian Mountains, among a group of people
who call themselves Melungeons.
ISBN 0-689-82007-0 (hc.)
[1. Orphans-fiction. 2. Melungeons-Fiction. 3. Identity-Fiction.
4. Appalachian Region-Fiction.] I. Title.
PZ7.N21San 1998
[Fic]-dc21
97-34067 CIP AC
ISBN 0-689-82006-2 (pbk.)

*To my editor, Jean Karl, for her insight,
my husband, Rex, for his critical eye,
Heather Wright, for her help with the research,
and to the Monday Night Group,
Larry Callen, Joan Carris, Marguerite
Murray, and Peggy Thomson,
who, as always, came through*

Melungeons (or Malungeons), people of mixed ancestry (American Indian and white, especially Portuguese, and sometimes black) living in remote mountain regions of n.e. Tennessee and w. Virginia . . . name probably derived from French *mélange* (mixture).

—*Compton's Interactive Encyclopedia,* 1995

one

ON a night even demons howl for their mothers, Josh stood on the edge of the highway, thumbing a ride.

The mountains were oblivious to summer, for the rain was so cold and the darkness so deep, Josh lost all track of time and place. He did not know whether the trucker had crossed from Pennsylvania into Maryland or whether he might have gone as far as Virginia. He'd said something about taking the route through Tennessee, but where was it he'd let Josh out? That's what came of nodding off. What Josh did know was that the four hundred dollars he had stashed beneath one sock squished in his shoe each time he shifted his weight, and the plastic bag he was using for rain gear was torn in places, next to useless.

"Damnation!"

It was more a description than a curse; the

landscape had the look of the lost. He truly had not expected this. The rain felt like sleet against his bare hands. He'd brought no gloves, no winter jacket, no cap other than an old Red Sox number, worn backward to keep the rain from running down his collar. And why should he have thought to bring them? It was August! Yet he was standing on a road cut through a cliff of shale, and the wind whistled like half-mad ghosts through the pass.

He knew it had been a mistake to hike up here. He should have gone with the trucker when he took the exit, and holed up at a gas station till he found another ride. Instead, Josh had asked the man to let him out when he made the turn, and had kept plodding along the shoulder of the highway, signaling to each approaching set of headlights; but no one stopped. It was later that the rain began, when the exits were great distances apart, the terrain forbidding.

Finally, noticing in the sweep of a trucker's headlights a narrow road heading up into the hills beyond the interstate, Josh had climbed over the guardrail, up the embankment, and had taken the strange roadway a mile at least, hoping to see the lights of a house or a town over the crest of the next hill. The blackness above, ahead, and below, however, seemed like a cosmic hole, sucking him in. He should have stayed on the interstate and taken his chances.

Only two cars had come this way in the past twenty minutes, tires smacking on the wet pavement. Neither stopped, neither slowed. The drivers probably couldn't see him in the darkness, with his black sneakers, blue jeans, and green plastic bag over his shoulders. He looked like the devil himself.

What if he died up here—hypothermia? Josh held his fingers to his face and blew on them. Should he turn back? Continue on? Go in whatever direction the next driver was heading, just to get warm? His teeth chattered violently as the wind whipped at the plastic and almost tore it off. This was crazy!

A few steps more—fifty feet, perhaps—and he might see a light. Then he would know whether to go on or turn back. He trudged forward, but the blackness only grew thicker, colder, the rain slashing him full in the face, matting his eyelashes.

Josh looked back uncertainly, and this time saw a faint glow on the rocky wall of the pass. He blinked. The glow grew brighter, then brighter still, until the rock was almost pink. Two headlights came into view. Josh stepped quickly out onto the pavement, wildly waving his arms, and his heart leaped when the vehicle began to slow.

It appeared to be an '89 Buick, maroon, perhaps—hard to tell because of the mud on the sides. Josh ran over and opened the door.

The light didn't work from the passenger side.

"Could I have a lift?" he called to the driver.

"Where you going?" a man's voice answered. In his thirties, maybe.

"Anyplace you are, weather like this."

Josh saw the man nod, so he opened the back door, shoved his pack onto the seat, then got in beside the driver. The warmth of the cushion was delicious, and he shivered involuntarily with the pleasure of it, carefully lifting the plastic bag over his head and shaking it on the floor in front of him.

"Heading anyplace in particular?" asked the stranger. The motor—clearly in need of maintenance—idled roughly.

"Dallas," Josh told him.

The man pulled onto the road again. "Where you from?"

"Boston." It wasn't Boston, actually, just a small town in the vicinity, but Josh liked the sound of it. He tried to make out the driver's face. A rough face, like the ride—pockmarked, thin-lipped, with bony cheeks and chin. The man didn't ask any more and Josh wondered if he should volunteer something else. He didn't feel like talking yet. "I'm going down there to live with my aunt," he offered finally.

"Long way to Texas. She didn't send any bus money?"

"I'm in no hurry to get there." Stupid

answer! Josh knew it as soon as the words were out—as though he had all the cash in the world just to bum around the country—so he added, "She doesn't have a lot of money. Neither do Mom and I." Did that sound convincing?

The driver made no reply, so Josh fixed his eyes on the night. The smell of his wet clothes filled the car. He was speaking of Mom in the present tense and that was strange, because six weeks ago the car accident had divided his life as though it was cut by a cleaver. Everything that had happened up to that point—the mother-and-son stuff—falling to one side, leaving him with only his future, which looked as gray and bleak and uncertain as the road ahead.

"You live in this part of the country?" he asked finally. The stranger's radio was off-station, a soft static with country music drifting through. Josh wondered why the man didn't either tune it or turn it off.

"Some miles up the road," the driver answered. His hand reached forward and turned the wipers on high, and they began a frenetic chopping kind of flip-flop.

"Where are we exactly?"

"Don't know it's got a name. Folks 'round here call it Sang Hollow."

"Well, I'm sure glad you picked me up. It's really cold for summer. I'll go as far as you're going on this road. If you could just let me off at a truck stop or gas station, though, I'd appreciate it."

"Be a while yet," the stranger said, and turned the radio up a little, static and all.

The reason the radio bothered Josh more than it might have was a reason he didn't want to think about, but did: the accident four blocks from home. Somehow Josh had known. Mom had said a quick good-bye as she'd left for work, and minutes later, he'd heard the crash—that heart-stopping sound of squealing tires—and then the impact, metal and glass.

He'd leaped up and gone outside without his shoes, the blood throbbing in his temples. Then he was running—running down the street in his stockinged feet like a lunatic—and far ahead at an intersection, he could see people gathering. Heard the wail of a siren off in the distance.

There was Mom's car, broadsided by a van. The door on the driver's side lay on the pavement. And there was Mom's dark curly hair on the seat, one arm dangling strangely over the steering wheel. The radio was still playing.

Now Josh sucked in his breath quickly, disguising it with a cough. The driver gave him a slow glance before turning his attention to the road again.

The car was almost too warm, and Josh felt

drowsy. The heater was malfunctioning, blowing a blast of hot air just below one knee, and Josh could feel his jeans drying in that spot, the stiffness of the fabric against his skin. His head began to nod and rolled to one side, but he jerked upright, only to feel his eyes closing again.

He dreamed that Aunt Carol was sitting behind him, telling him that Mom hadn't died after all. That she was waiting for him to call her, in fact. He had laughed with relief and said, "Turn off the radio, then." And Josh opened his eyes to see the stranger at the wheel, darkness coming at them through the windshield, and once again, disappointment ballooned inside his chest as it had for the past six weeks each time he wakened. The never-ending sadness. He let his body sink back into the comfort of the seat, wanting to escape again into dreams.

How was it possible, he kept asking himself, that a single two-second incident, a sudden turn by the driver of the van, could change his life so completely? That the future—*his* future—could be altered so radically by a person he didn't even know, and end his mom's future altogether?

Things had been going extraordinarily well. He was due to get his driver's license in another five months and, after he graduated, he planned to go to Boston U. and then apply for medical school. If he could get in, and get financial help, he wanted to go into sports medicine. Now this.

Josh hadn't realized how few relatives he had. No grandparents left on either side, and Mom's only sister was both divorced and diabetic. Josh had been added to her problems.

Aunt Carol had flown to Boston, of course, to help with funeral arrangements and to get the house ready for sale. What else could she do before she flew back to Dallas but tell Josh he was welcome to live with her? And what could he do but say yes?

What had happened was that a friend invited him to go backpacking along the Appalachian Trail the first three weeks of August, so Josh told Aunt Carol he'd fly out to her place on the twenty-fourth. But the more he thought of carrying his anger and sadness along on his friend's vacation, the more he felt like odd man out. So he told his friend he was flying to Aunt Carol's instead. And then, he realized suddenly, he was free. It brought no relief, however. Only the knowledge that he wouldn't have to deal with anyone but himself for a while. That was pain enough.

He'd stuffed the plane ticket in his pack, stashed four hundred dollars in one shoe, then set off to hitchhike to Texas and get there in his own time. No one would know.

Josh could not come to terms with time. If

Mom had only reached the intersection a moment earlier . . . If the van had only been a few seconds later . . . He kept trying to relive it, change it, filter it through a time warp of some sort so that he could erase the accident and get on with his life. Yet his future had come to a standstill.

The car seemed to be slowing, and Josh opened his eyes. The Buick was veering off to the right, two wheels traveling the bumpy shoulder until at last it came to a stop. Josh put his face close to the side window, but saw only darkness.

"This is as far as you go," the stranger said.

"Where are we?"

"Told you. Sang Hollow."

"We were in Sang Hollow an hour ago!"

"It's here and about."

Josh began to wonder if they'd been going around in circles. All he'd succeeded in doing was getting his clothes half dry. "Any gas station where I could wait for a ride?" he asked.

"None that I know of."

Trying to hide his irritation, Josh reached for the door handle. "Well, I'll give it a try. Thanks for the lift," he said dully.

"You owe me." The stranger's voice caught him off guard, so low he almost missed it. Cold as rain.

"What?" Josh turned in his seat.

"You owe me something. I came twenty miles out of my way."

"For what? I'm still out in the boonies, not a town in sight. You should have told me you were charging."

"I'm tellin' you now."

"Look. I don't have much on me. I've got to make it to Dallas."

He was jerked forward so suddenly that he almost bumped heads with the driver.

"Don't give me that, Boston boy," the man said, hand clutching Josh's collar so close to the throat that it was hard for him to breathe. "You wearin' hundred-dollar shoes and jacket."

It wasn't true, but what difference did it make?

"H-how much do I owe you?" Josh said, surprised at the man's strength.

"All you got."

Josh reared backward, catching the stranger by surprise. Freeing one hand, he pushed open the door. He stumbled out and yanked his pack from the backseat. The driver sprang from his side of the car and was on him faster than he could blink, pummeling him blow after blow.

A fist smashed him full in the face and he was down.

A boot caught him squarely in the ribs, and he was out.

two

BLOOD. Josh could taste it. Smell it. He lay on his side, his left cheek pressed against the earth, the icy rain pinging on his face. The place where the fist had connected with his nose and upper lip was still blessedly numb. He tried to sit up.

There was a breath-choking stab in his rib cage. Josh cried out and rolled over on his back. Every breath sent a spasm of pain through him. He knew he could not stay where he was, but wasn't at all sure he could stand, much less walk. His feet felt unusually cold, and when he wiggled his toes, he realized that his shoes were gone, and the four hundred dollars along with them. So were his jacket and wallet.

He groaned. His fingers sought out his wrist and discovered that his watch was missing. Moving one hand along the zipper of his pack, he fumbled around inside. The plane ticket was still there. A second pair of jeans. Underwear. Sweatshirt. So were his old sneakers with the hole in one toe. But his Walkman was gone. The only thing he could say for the creep who robbed him was that he hadn't killed him, too.

Think survival, he told himself. It was the first time in his life he'd been really tested. He knew that he had to keep his body moving, keep it warm, and find shelter.

Once more Josh struggled to sit up, bracing himself with both hands. His nose began to throb now. But it was the sharp pain in his rib cage that ordered him to the ground again.

If I can't get up, he thought, *I'll die.* He experimented with keeping his upper body as rigid as possible. With elbows and hands braced under him, he inched himself upward into a sitting position. Finally, clutching his pack so he would not have to bend over again, he began the long, torturous task of getting to his feet. Next problem: He could not put on his sneakers. This he knew without even trying. He could not lean down without feeling the boot again in his ribs.

Mercifully the rain was slackening. Step by step, Josh moved along the road in his stockinged feet. He knew he was incapable of making any kind of shelter for himself with pain as severe as his. How could it be so cold? It was as though the rain had come from a different sky, another season. He hobbled on. Every road led somewhere, so why not stick to this one, narrow as it was?

Josh managed to get his sweatshirt out of his pack, but putting it on was the most painful procedure yet. When he finally succeeded and set out again, he was surprised to discover that the road was unpaved. The man who had picked him up must have driven a long way out in the country before he robbed him. Josh still had seventy dollars in his money belt (it used to be Dad's, Mom had said) and a nonrefundable plane ticket. He groaned again as a slight misstep threw his body off balance momentarily. He was destined, it seemed, to relive the kick over and over.

All was blackness around him except for the sky, where he could just make out a hint of moon now, a ring of silver. Not fifty feet in front of him, however, off on the shoulder, he saw something else, small clumps of white on the ground—discarded clothing, perhaps. But as Josh drew closer, he saw that they were rocks, outlining a rectangle. Inside the rectangle, more rocks had been placed in the shape of a body, and at the head of the configuration stood a small white cross.

Fear swept over him, more devastating than his being robbed. He knew there were places on the continent so remote that people were buried where they fell, but he could not imagine being in an area that isolated. How long since he'd left the interstate? Two hours? Three?

A sound. Josh stood still as a stone, listening. It was a rhythmical kind of noise that reminded him of a clock pendulum. Then he realized it was the hoofbeats of a horse, accompanied by the soft creak and grind of wheels.

He would take his chances. There was nothing much left to steal. Josh moved out into the middle of the muddy road in his socks and stood waiting, face turned in the direction of the sound.

A horse came into view—dappled, with splotches of gray. It was pulling a wagon with lanterns swinging at either side. A woman sat at the reins. It seemed incongruous here, but so had the other events of the night. He waited, his features bunched up in pain, as the horse drew near. It slowed but did not stop until the wagon was right beside the spot where Josh was standing.

The woman was of indeterminate age, her head and shoulders covered by a coarse brown shawl. Her face was indistinct in the light of the lanterns, round, with shadows.

"I'm hurt," Josh called, "and I need a ride to wherever you're going."

She motioned wordlessly to the wagon in back, sensing, perhaps, that he could not make the climb up on the bench beside her. With great difficulty, Josh heaved his pack on some burlap sacks in the wagon, groaning audibly as he did so, and then he simply lay forward, hunching as far as he could onto the bed of the wagon, feet dangling. The horse began to move again, and Josh was in and out of sleep.

Silence all around him. The last noise he had heard was the wagon wheels and the clip-clop of hooves. An occasional snort from the animal, anxious to get where it was going. Now there was the kind of quiet that carries a presence with it, and without even opening his eyes, Josh knew that someone was nearby.

"We could always kill him."

Josh felt his pulse soar, his legs stiffen.

"For what good?"

"If he doesn't return, someone would come. They'd have to investigate."

"We don't have to kill him to keep him here, Kaspar." A third voice. Josh wondered how many people were present. "You didn't return, and no one's come for you."

"Nor for Jack, when he died. We dug his grave ourselves," said someone else.

Josh cautiously opened his eyes, and in the light of a lantern, found a half dozen faces peering down at him—swarthy young men mostly, and another of indeterminate age.

"He's awake."

Josh struggled to sit up, and did so at last, hugging his rib cage. He was still on a pile of empty sacks in the back of a wagon, which was parked now in what appeared to be a stable. The horse, unharnessed, was feeding in a nearby stall.

"I'm Pardo," the older man said to him. "Where are you from?"

Josh felt his dry lips stick together at the corners as he tried to speak. He ran his tongue over them. "Massachusetts. I was hitchhiking to Texas to live with my aunt." He studied the people around him and, though he had never seen them before, had the feeling he was looking through old family photos. "Some guy picked me up on the road out there, then jumped me and stole my money. He took my shoes and jacket, too. I think he might have broken one of my ribs when he kicked me." Josh pointed to his left side.

"Cracked, like as not," Pardo said.

"What I need is to get to an airport." Josh winced as he tried to slide off the wagon, then gave up.

"No airport around here," Pardo told him. "I can tape up those ribs for you, though. Make you feel better."

Josh looked about, agitated at the amused smiles on some of the faces. "How far are we from the interstate?"

"That's a ways, too," Pardo replied, not unkindly. Somebody laughed.

Josh closed his eyes again and let his head droop. He was almost too tired to think. Kill him, don't kill him, what did it matter? His face was swollen, his nose throbbed, his upper lip was thick and his body sore. The next time he looked around, the place was empty.

Pardo soon returned, however, with long strips of linen, and helped Josh strip to the waist. He examined Josh's ribs with his fingers to see if there was any protrusion of bone, then instructed him to let out his breath and hold it while he quickly bound his chest. When Josh breathed in, he explained, expanding his rib cage, the strapping would hold the cracked bone together, enabling it to heal faster.

Josh studied the coppery face, the ageless eyes, a deep blue. It was impossible to estimate how old the man was. One moment Josh guessed he was ancient, yet at other times he seemed almost young.

When the procedure was over, Pardo helped him slide off the wagon and made a bed of burlap and straw on the floor. Josh lay down on his back and let out his breath. When he drew it in again, he found that the strapping did help somewhat. Pardo, however, was gone.

He was hungry, but too tired to go in search of food. Thirsty, but not enough to reawaken the pain in his ribs. The burlap on which he lay was warm under his body, the air pungent with the scent of hay and horse manure. So Josh took the easiest way out and slept.

It was a restless sleep, broken at times by dreams—regret and sadness and an innate longing for his mother, for the easy, casual, untroubled life they'd had before. He woke once in the middle of the night and went through the excruciating ritual of rolling over, then bracing his body with one hand and rising to a sitting position. Once on his feet, he tottered outside to relieve himself, then made his way back to the spot on the floor where the burlap welcomed him once again. This time he slept in earnest.

At dawn, he was aware of activity in the stable—the soft crunch of footsteps, the clunk of a saddle being hoisted off a hook, the rustle of reins . . .

Josh opened his eyes halfway, the bronze light of early morning filtering through his lashes. Pardo was working to untangle a harness, murmuring to an animal that Josh heard and smelled, but could not see. Lying motionless on the burlap, his clothes still damp in places from the previous night's rain, Josh studied the thick-tipped fingers of the man, the coarse gray garment he wore over his trousers, the deep furrows in his face. If he wasn't old, Josh decided, he was so ravaged by weather that he seemed himself a piece of the landscape—sod and wheat and rain and frost.

From time to time others came and left, carrying large woven pouches slung over their shoulders, sticks in hand. Occasionally a female voice broke the stillness, and the next time Josh opened his eyes, a large-framed girl a year or two older than he looked down at him, a bemused smile on her face. She wore a man's rough shirt, tucked loosely in the top of her baggy trousers, her long hair pulled back from her forehead and fastened with a comb.

Josh felt as though he had been caught snoring, and snapped his jaws together.

"You're the one Leone found at the pass," she guessed. "We heard."

He nodded and pushed himself up on his elbow, then ran one hand through his hair. "Look. I'm Josh Vardy, and I need to get to an airport no matter how far away it is."

The girl studied him. She wasn't as tall as Josh, but she appeared strong, and simply ignored what he said. "Hungry?" she asked.

"Yes. Starved. I would have slept longer if my stomach wasn't making so much noise. What's your name?"

"Mavis." Her face was round like that of the woman named Leone, but her cheekbones were more prominent. "Old Sly will make you work for every bite you take."

"Only breakfast, and I'm outta here."

She jeered. "You can hardly sit up without groaning. How will you travel?"

"Hitchhike."

"To there and back!" Mavis scoffed. And then, "Stay here. I'll bring you a biscuit." She disappeared.

Josh managed to get himself to his feet before the girl returned. She held a tin cup full of milk and a flat piece of bread, spread heavily with clotted cream. It would have been nauseating to Josh if he weren't so hungry.

"Thank you," he said, and tried not to wolf it down. "Anyone around here have a car?"

"Not here."

"Where, then?"

"Farther along than this."

"Look. I think I'd like to stay one more day till I can move around easier. Could I pay for some food and just crash till my rib is better?"

She looked puzzled at his expression, and then, understanding, said, "It's up to you." Slipping her pouch over her shoulder, she left.

When he had drunk the last of the milk, Josh slowly got to his feet and surveyed his surroundings. He was in a long building of rough-hewn logs, with stalls along one side, hay at both ends, and enough room to park two wagons. He made his way over to the door of the stable and looked out over the rural landscape. A scent he could not name teased his nostrils, then wafted away again, so subtle he could almost have missed it. It was nothing he had smelled before, and he wasn't entirely sure it was an odor at all. An aura perhaps.

Everything was sealed in fog—a hut, a shed, a wagon, a well. Everything was gray—gray sky, gray trees, gray hut, gray ground. Gray people in gray clothes moving about the clearing, and there was no sound at all now but the drip, drip of water off one corner of the roof, splashing slowly, one drop at a time, into a large barrel.

Josh longed for a drink and moved a step at a time over to the rain barrel. But when he looked down into the cold gray water, he discovered that the ripples did not spread outward from where a drop had just landed, but started instead at the edge of the barrel, the circles growing smaller and smaller until the surface glazed over once again.

three

THE broken rib, he decided, was something he could live with. Josh remembered his basketball coach telling him that a cracked rib healed itself—the game against Medford, when Josh scored seventeen points in the second half. He had thought he'd broken a rib, but he hadn't. *This* was a broken rib. As he ambled cautiously about, however, he found that the pain he felt when he made a wrong move was as bad as it would get, and after reconciling himself to that, he began to think of traveling on.

Somewhere there had to be a Hardee's. At least a roadside café. He doubted he could make his seventy dollars last till he reached Texas, unless he lucked out and got a trucker who was driving straight through. But that sort of defeated the whole idea—to have at least one adventure he could talk about when he walked into his new school. Everything he'd been back home—track star, basketball center, swimmer—he was leaving behind, and his junior year, which would have been one of his best, would find him in a larger school in a distant city, a nobody now who had to start all over. This little trek getting down there was supposed to be his ace in the hole:

You moved here from Boston?
Hitchhiked, actually.
No kidding? How long did it take?
Couple weeks.
Where'd you sleep?
Well, it's a long story . . .

As he moved away from the stable where he had spent the night, he became aware of other sounds—an ax chopping, a rooster boasting, wheels turning, carts creaking—low, everyday working noises.

Josh had headed in the direction of a thin curl of smoke he saw rising above the treetops when he realized just how battered and sore he really was. It was possible he had more than a broken rib, and he was about to sit down on a stump to rest when he saw a small cabin in the trees ahead, about as primitive as he could imagine. He could only believe that he had come upon one of the deepest hollows in one of the most remote places in Appalachia.

No one seemed to be at home, but Josh knocked anyway. He was surprised when a small wooden window opened in the door and he found his face within inches of a bearded man with copper skin and blue eyes, similar to Pardo's. Despite the beard, his skin had few wrinkles. He could be fifty—forty, even—but the eyes! The eyes seemed to go back, back, through age after age—centuries, even.

"Hello," said Josh, but the eyes never blinked. "Could you tell me if there's anyplace I could get a sandwich?" When the man made no response, Josh said, "Is there a restaurant nearby?"

In answer, the man spoke in a language Josh did not recognize. It could have been Spanish, but the only word the man kept repeating was "Portyghee." And then, before Josh could question him further, the window closed.

"No sandwich here, that's for sure," Josh muttered to himself as he went back down the lane again, following the deep ruts of wagon wheels in the mud.

He passed a second cabin and then a third before he stopped suddenly and looked about with a new appreciation of his predicament. There were ruts of wagon wheels in the unpaved road, and the dents of horses' hooves, but no tire tracks at all. Neither were there, along the way, any telephone poles.

"Waaaay out in the boonies!" Josh decided.

Every dwelling was made of logs, so that the

place had the look of a summer camp or an early settlement. The smaller buildings—springhouses, perhaps—were more mud than logs. Everything, even the carts and wheelbarrows, appeared to be made by hand.

His nose was bleeding again, the blood running backward down his throat, and his fatigue made him slightly nauseated. Josh decided to give up exploring for now, and made his way back to the stable, to the pile of burlap and straw, and, for want of anything better to do, he slept.

When he woke this time, he was ravenous, and stood in the doorway waiting for whoever would show. The fog had lifted, and Josh was surprised to see that there were hills, layers of hills, rising high above the trees. He had thought when he left the interstate that he had climbed and climbed to the place he had been robbed. Perhaps the woman in the cart had taken him down again to a valley on the other side, for a valley it seemed to be. Or perhaps the valley where she had taken him was a hollow high in the mountains, and he would have to go through a pass and down the other side before he could get back to the highway. Up or down? Down or up? He was thoroughly confused.

Josh heard the sound of the horse and wagon long before they came into view. This time, however, the moon-faced woman was not alone. A dozen or so people sat in the back, and a minute later they all piled out, the strangely shaped pouches slung over their shoulders.

It was a diverse group, male and female. The older women wore long skirts, but the younger seemed to prefer the trousers of the men—clothes of a cut and cloth unfamiliar to him. The garments were earth-colored, and so were most of the people, from the olive hue of old leaves to the dusky tones of clay. Their delicate features seemed to have been drawn with a fine-tipped pen, and though many had brown eyes, in keeping with their skin, a surprising number of eyes were blue, like Josh's. Like Pardo's. Josh had always wondered why, with as Boston Irish a mother as one could imagine, he himself looked Italian. His skin turned red-brown when he tanned.

The workers were talking among themselves, getting into line at the far end of the stable to have their pouches weighed and recorded, and though most were speaking English, a few of the older ones, like the man in the cabin, had a dialect Josh couldn't decipher, and a beard to go with it. There was the clink of silver as each worker was paid according to the weight of his pouch. Josh sought out the driver, who was unharnessing her horse.

"I want to thank you for picking me up last night," he said. "I was in pretty bad shape."

The moon-faced woman gave him a nod and lifted the bridle from the horse's head.

"I really need to be on my way as soon as possible," Josh continued. "My aunt's expecting me. If you could take me out to the road on your next trip . . ."

The woman made no answer, but a second female, large and sturdy, answered for her, untying the kerchief from around her head: "Welcome, Josh. Leone is mute. She can hear, but she doesn't speak."

"Oh, I'm sorry. I was wondering if I could ride with her on her next trip out. I have to get to Dallas," Josh explained.

The woman shook out her head scarf and tucked it in a pocket. "The way in is not the way out," she said.

"Well, what *is* the way out, then? If you'll just point me in the right direction, I can probably walk it," Josh said.

"That I don't know," the woman replied, and then, more brightly, "I'm Eulaylia. Would you like some supper?"

Josh felt his patience going. "Now wait a minute," he said, following her as she left the barn. "Leone picked me up. She must have been coming from somewhere."

"Eh, but you won't be going where Leone has been," the woman said. "Come on, Josh. You must be hungry. Follow the others to the cookhouse, and tell Old Sly I sent you."

Josh leaned for a moment against the door of the stable. Any moment he expected his mind to rise from sleep. He could almost see himself beginning to smile, sorting out this ridiculous dream. But the pain in his rib cage was real. So was the ache in his nose and the hunger in his gut.

Just do what they say and keep your eyes open, he told himself.

He had not seen Mavis come in with the others, but then a second wagon turned into the clearing, and the girl climbed down with the rest of the crew.

Josh walked over. "Hello, again. Eulaylia says I'm invited to dinner."

"Feeling any better?"

"Not a whole lot, but at least I can move around."

The muscular young man they had called Kaspar, who had been in the stable the night before, walked over. "Anyone out there looking for you?" he asked Josh.

Josh decided to play it cagey. "Out where?"

"Beyond. This aunt you were talking of last night. Will she be missing you yet?"

"Not quite," Josh answered, then wondered if he'd made a mistake. "But she will soon," he added.

"How soon?" The thing Josh noticed about

Kaspar was his teeth. Strong, white teeth—the incisors sharp as picks. "What about your parents?"

"Mom died in a car crash in June. I'm going to live with my aunt in Texas." Hard to figure out what the right answers were supposed to be, so why not tell the truth? "Dad died when I was a baby," he added.

"I'm sorry," Mavis told him.

"And now, well, I wanted to just stay in our house near Boston, but the court says you need a guardian till you're eighteen." Josh shrugged. "I even asked one of my friends if I could stay at his place for my last two years of high school, but his folks didn't think much of the idea."

"So why wouldn't your aunt be looking for you now?" Kaspar asked, impatient with the story.

"Because I wanted to take my time getting down there—get my head together. Figured I could hitchhike."

"Stupid," said Kaspar.

Josh felt his back stiffen. "Maybe," he said.

He waited outside while Mavis and Kaspar had their sacks weighed at the back of the stable, then walked with them to the center of the village—not as far as he had thought—and to a large low building where smoke came out of a chimney at either end. Inside, women were cooking at each fireplace, and in between were long tables and benches that reminded Josh of summer camp in New Hampshire—the smell of overcooked food, musty rafters, strong soap . . .

They joined some others at one of the tables, directly across from a younger boy named Gil. The company was mixed, old as well as young. The elders, Josh noticed, gave him welcoming smiles, but the younger ones were simply curious.

"This the table for enlisted men?" Josh joked before he sat down, trying for levity. And when Gil smiled, he asked, "What is this place, anyway? Boot camp?"

They studied him quizzically.

"I mean, am I in for the duration or what? Is this the way you get workers? Pick up the mugged out on the road and add them to the workforce?"

"No one gets here the same way," Kaspar told him. "That goes for getting out, too."

Josh looked up. "Then it's not a life sentence?"

But Mavis's reply did not particularly cheer him. "Sometimes not," she said.

The food was largely unfamiliar, whether because of what it was or the way it was cooked: He recognized potatoes, beets, and onions, but they were all mixed together with vegetables he did not know. There was also chicken or pork, it was hard to tell, served with tomato gravy. The bread was set out in long loaves, and everyone simply grasped the loaf with both hands, still grungy from work, and tore off a piece. Josh did the same.

He could best describe the meal as pungent. It was not the taste he was conscious of as much as the odor—of vegetables somewhat burnt and badly seasoned. It blended with the smell of bodies, sweaty with the day's exertions, a mildew odor, just like the cabins he remembered as a young boy.

He was about to ask another question when someone asked one of him. Josh felt a rough hand on his shoulder and turned to see a large man whose face seemed older than his body. His complexion was ruddy, the skin lined as old leather. He had flowing gray hair and beard, and bushy brows, beneath which black eyes stared intently, as though from the mouths of caves.

"Who are you?" he thundered. "And how did you get here?"

four

JOSH swallowed, and immediately choked on a bit of carrot. When he coughed, the pain in his chest was excruciating.

"Eulaylia sent me," he said, hugging his ribs as he coughed again.

"When did you get here? Leone brought you in?"

"Yes. I was mugged out on the road and she found me. I've got a broken rib."

"You will work," said the man.

"Old Sly, go easy," one of the elders called.

"I'll be glad to do whatever I can. Where shall I sleep?" Josh asked.

"Where did you spend last night?"

"In the stable."

"Then that's where you'll stay," the big man said, and moved on.

Josh turned to Mavis. "The kingpin?"

"I don't know your word," she said, puzzled.

"The big cheese. The boss."

"We all work; Sly, too. He's my grandfather."

"Does he treat all new recruits the same way?"

Mavis smiled. "He's gruff. It's his manner. As for the stable, all the cottages and bunkhouses are full. We haven't room here to build more cabins. What level land we have is needed for planting."

Josh tried to take it all in. "Then why don't you expand—spread out into another valley?"

"I'm afraid that's not possible," she said, and bit into her bread.

Josh waited for her to explain, but she did not continue the discussion, so he asked, "What kind of work do you do?"

"Any work there is. But the digging season has just begun. Whoever can be spared goes digging."

"Potatoes?" Josh said, looking around.

This time the boy named Gil answered. "'Sang."

"Excuse me?"

"Ginseng," Kaspar told him. "Here it's called 'sang."

"Some kind of vegetable?"

Gil seemed to think this particularly funny, and laughed loudly, but he appeared to be a genial sort of boy who laughed easily.

"It's a plant, and we harvest the root,"

Mavis explained. "Wild ginseng is scarce and very valuable, and Appalachia is one of the few places on earth you can find it in any quantity."

"So that's where we are? The Appalachians?"

"Where did you think?" Kaspar sneered.

Josh wasn't sure what he thought. Another planet, perhaps. The Planet of Weirdness. "Who buys the ginseng?" he asked.

"Chinese traders," said Mavis.

"What? Where do they sell it?"

"They market it in the Orient."

"What's it used for?"

"Everything," Gil told him, smiling still. "Tea, tonic, even ginseng jelly. Whatever you've got wrong with you, ginseng will cure, they say. I drank the tea once. It was awful."

Everyone was eating so much, so fast, that Josh began to wonder if this was the last meal they would get for a while. Although he didn't care for the taste of scorched vegetables and overcooked meat, he remembered his hunger of that morning and forced the food down, even slipping a piece of bread in his pocket for later.

"How will I know what it looks like?" he asked Kaspar. "I've never dug ginseng before."

"I'll show you, and more besides," Kaspar murmured.

Mavis said, "Look for a plant about two feet tall with small fingerlike leaves and bright red berries. It's the looking, though, that's difficult."

"And after digging season, you all go home?" Josh asked hopefully.

Gil laughed gleefully, slapping the edge of the table. "This *is* home," he said. "I've been here all my life."

Coldness ran through Josh's veins.

Mavis said: "After the digging season, we repair the cabins, store the food, weave, butcher the pigs, settle in for winter, and wait until next season. In spring there are lambs to birth, sheep to shear, corn to plant. There's always work to be done. If we don't grow it or catch it, we don't eat. That's a fact."

Dread, almost as deadly as the fear Josh had felt earlier, overtook him.

"Listen," he said earnestly, glancing around the table at anyone who would hear him out. "I'll be glad to work as long as I'm here. But I've got to get to my aunt in Texas. She's not well, and I'm going to help her out." Since when had he given any real thought to his aunt? It embarrassed him, the way he was using her now. "I didn't mean to come here and be a burden or anything. If you'll just tell me what road to take, I'll work tomorrow, then leave."

He was surprised when the whole table broke into laughter. For most, like Gil, it was hearty and strong, but in the eyes of the elders there was a sympathy he could not overlook.

"So go," said a young man named Chad, and everyone laughed again.

"Which way?"

"There's only one road, and it ends at the barn," somebody told him, and seemed not to realize how ridiculous it sounded.

"And if I follow it in the other direction, where will it take me?" Josh asked.

"To The Edge," Gil said.

"Come again? The edge of what?"

Gil shrugged. "I don't know, I've never been."

The conversation was too frustrating to continue. Bizarre, that's what it was. An argument had broken out at the other end of the table as to whether someone had dug up a plant that morning that was too young, and soon diners began to leave, placing their earthenware plates and cups in a soapy tub by the door. Josh followed and did the same.

Outside, the women moved one way, men the other. Josh soon discovered that the women went to an outdoor pump off in the trees to wash, and the men walked to the river. Heaven knew he needed a bath. He could feel blood still encrusted in one nostril, blood in his hair. His nose, he could tell, was swollen.

It was a setting that seemed medieval—workers in their earth-colored pants and shirts, filing down past the cow barn toward the river. That scent again! From one of the cabins off to the side came a warm glow from the window—a flickering light from a kerosene lamp, perhaps, or a fireplace. Josh wasn't sure. As they passed the barn he could hear the soft crunch of cows' teeth chewing hay. Here and there a villager went from garden to hut, from barn to well—drawing water, emptying pots, sweeping a doorstep, wheeling a cart. Had no one heard of the Industrial Revolution? he wondered. They could all have emerged from an Old World painting.

Josh decided, as he took off his clothes with the others and dropped them on the bank, that this was an isolated community, so far back in the hills that there was almost no contact with the outside. They had made their living for decades—centuries, perhaps—doing for themselves, but as the younger people grew up and left the community one by one, they were in constant need of more workers, and once a stranger stumbled into their midst, they were loath to let him go.

Well, he was going. If Leone came in with the wagon, she went out with the wagon, and it didn't matter to Josh if they were fifty miles back in the hollows, he'd follow those wagon wheel ruts to wherever they led.

As he bathed himself with the crude bar of

homemade soap that was passed from one man to another, he couldn't help but be envious of Kaspar's naked body, as strong as a tiger's, the muscles on his arms bulging like bags of potatoes. Josh's own frame was lean, but at least he was strong and swift. Basketball and track had seen to that. He had no doubt that if he just knew the way out, he'd make it.

Little was said at the river. The water wasn't warm, for one thing. With those steep wooded hills on either side, the sun was a long time coming in the mornings, he guessed, and soon after it reached the water, it was slipping behind the trees once more.

None of the older men seemed especially curious about him, Old Sly excepted. Most were probably fatigued from the day's work. The younger men glanced at him now and then, amused at the way his chest was taped, but to Josh it meant the difference between moving around at all or lying on a heap of burlap for the next couple of weeks.

The elders did their bathing, then climbed the bank to dress and go on home. Pardo did stop long enough to ask if Josh felt any better, and Josh was grateful for that small kindness. The young men stayed in the water a while longer, splashing each other and diving like ducks, but no one ventured out beyond a certain point.

Josh did not venture at all. Knowing he was to go to work the following day with the others, he shuffled back to the stable, past the small cottages that were the domain of the older folk, he noticed, and the long bunkhouses where the younger men slept. The young women, he observed, still seemed to live at home. He eased himself down on the straw, too weary to unpack his bedroll. No, he thought, it wasn't only that. To unpack meant he was going to stay a while, and he had no intention of staying. The sooner he left, the better.

He opened his mouth and let a long slow sigh escape. To sneeze was disaster. He was surprised at how tired he felt for the little exertion he had put in that day, and guessed that the effort of simply getting himself around without a major spasm was all he could manage. As twilight fell upon him, he listened to the *ha-chunk* of a pump handle, to the slosh of water on the ground, to voices beyond the stable, and to the twitterings and calls of birds settling down for the evening in the rafters. To nighthawks foraging for prey.

Weary as he was, he didn't fall asleep as readily as he had hoped. Kaspar's remark to the others the night before about killing him was disturbing, not because Josh took it seriously, but because it upset his theory. If workers were needed, Old Sly and Kaspar would hardly be trying to scare them off. They might threaten to kill him should he try to leave, perhaps, but not for having arrived. The others, for the most part, were kind. Something didn't make sense here. A *lot* didn't make sense.

He slept at last. He must have, because he dreamed he was dreaming. Dreamed that all that had happened was a nightmare from which he had now awakened—that he was home in his own bedroom, and his mother was standing in the doorway smiling at him as he turned over in bed and saw her there.

"I *told* you I'd be back, didn't I?" she was saying in the dream, and he stumbled out of bed, laughing, joyous. Except that he still heard her car radio playing, as it had at the crash. Then the song ended and there was only static. Loud static, and he wondered why she didn't just turn it off.

And then he realized it wasn't static at all. It was barking, and the barking seemed to be growing more and more frenzied.

His eyes suddenly opened, and Josh first had to swim through his grief and disappointment at discovering his mother truly gone. Slowly the dullness and flatness of his awakening gave way to curiosity, for he hadn't remembered seeing any dogs in the village. Was there a neighboring town, perhaps? All this time, were they right next door to a little hamlet that might just possibly have a phone?

Then he heard footsteps—running footsteps—voices, and saw the light from bobbing lanterns passing by the windows of the stable. Darkness closed in again, the voices grew more indistinct, until finally even the footsteps faded away.

The barking stopped as suddenly as it had begun, and Josh hadn't the energy to get up and find out why.

five

THE one advantage—the only advantage—of the last two days was that it had kept him focused on survival. Now that he had a place to sleep in comparative safety, food, and people around him, however strange, he rediscovered grief. Or perhaps grief found him. As though a window had opened and a cold wind rushed through.

If his mind roamed free for just a moment, it would play out the accident again and again. An ordinary day—Mom heading for the office, Josh getting ready for his last track meet of the semester. Only a week left of school, then he and Mom were supposed to leave for a Maine vacation. All destroyed in five seconds or less—a thoroughly preventable accident.

Over and over, he tried to remember his last words to her that morning. That was the awful part: He couldn't. There had been no argument.

Of that he was sure, so he didn't have something like that on his conscience. Probably she'd asked what time he'd be home, whether she should make dinner or pick something up. He'd undoubtedly said he'd be home after six. Whatever they'd said or left unspoken, it was the usual mundane chatter. If only he'd known . . .

He could have told her he loved her, admired her for the way she'd raised him alone all these years, for the sacrifices she'd made. But what guy goes around thanking his mom each day, expecting it to be her last? If *he* had been the one in the accident, Aunt Carol had reminded him, Mom's last words to him would have been ordinary, too.

He knew that. And even though the police told him she had died instantly, it didn't help much. Because in the moment she had lost her life, Josh had lost his—the life he had known, anyway. He had lost his mother, his home, his school, his community . . . There was scarcely an edition of the high school paper that didn't mention Josh Vardy's name somewhere—a prize won, a photo, a quote. Girls had begun calling his number, and he'd started going out. Even though he was a big fish in a very small pond and he knew it, life was good. And now . . .

But mostly it was just missing Mom. Missing her voice, her laugh, the way she gave his back a few quick caresses when they hugged. She'd always been there for him—his games, his meets; he had never imagined a time when she wouldn't be. And now that time was here, and Josh drew himself into a fetal position, burying his face in the burlap.

He lay for some time until finally hunger drove him to get up and dress. He longed for the usual breakfast he made for himself the day of an evening swim meet—a huge stack of pancakes, triple the syrup, a bowl of Wheat Chex, maybe, a banana shake. Longed for Mom to be sitting across the table from him, watching him eat, making jokes, laughing her tinkling laugh.

Josh took clean underwear from his pack, slowly pulled on his jeans, mindful of the pain in his rib cage, and tied his shoes. He was so deep in thought that he did not notice Old Sly in one of the stalls, harnessing the dappled mare, until the man spoke to him.

"I want you to be watchful of Kaspar," he said. And when Josh looked at him, wondering, added, "He's not to be trusted."

"Then why let him work for you?"

"We work for the shoes we wear and the tools we use to dig. But Kaspar's impatient. He's a stripper, and cares not a copper penny for what he leaves behind."

"I don't know what you're talking about, so I'm afraid I won't be much help," said Josh.

Old Sly turned his stout frame around in the

narrow stall, then came out and motioned for Josh to follow. At the other end of the stable, the man bent down and, grunting slightly, reached into one of the pouches, taking out what appeared to be, at first glance, a small home-made doll, roughly carved from wood. When he handed it over, however, Josh saw that it was a gnarled brown root, about six inches long, with appendages something like those of the human body. Josh sniffed at the root, and though there wasn't much scent, wondered if this perhaps was the smell he had detected earlier.

"Ginseng?" he guessed.

Old Sly nodded. "'Sang," he replied, with a kind of reverence. Nudging Josh out the side door, he directed him across the clearing to a path that led to the woods. After they had walked a while through a tall stand of oak and hickory, Old Sly left the path, parting the branches and carefully watching where he put his feet. Finally he pointed to a plant about two feet tall with whorls of leaves at the top, and bright red berries.

"This is the way she grows," he said. "This is the way you'll spot her—by the berries. You dig the roots from only the larger stalks, and spare the smaller two- and three-pronged plants. If you dig the roots before the berries have a chance to ripen, they won't make seed, and the ginseng will die out."

Josh should have cared, but didn't. There was nothing that interested him less at this point than the future of ginseng. He was interested in his own future, if he had one. It was important, however, for him to get along this one day so he could leave.

Old Sly was talking again. "That's Kaspar, I'm thinking—digging the roots he's no business taking—strippers, we call the ones who do that. Be watchful."

Why was he telling *him* this? Josh wondered. As they headed back to the stable, he thought he heard dogs barking again, far off in the distance.

"What was all the commotion last night?" he asked.

At first Old Sly didn't answer, but when Josh waited, he said, "Commotion?"

"All the dogs. The barking."

"I heard no barking," Old Sly told him.

Joshua stared. "You *must* have. There were footsteps and voices right outside my window. People went to investigate."

"I sleep like the dead," replied Old Sly, and that was the end of it. Josh followed him on to the cookhouse, where he smelled, once again, scorching, this time of breakfast. He was glad when he saw Mavis break away from the small group of women she was walking with and wait for him. She sang softly as if to amuse herself, turning her body from side to side and clapping silently, until he caught up with her. Then she stopped.

"You look awful," she said, but her eyes were laughing.

"I do? I feel a little better, actually. Why? What's wrong?"

"Your bruises are turning purple. Your left eye's every color of the rainbow, in fact."

"Well, it's a sign of healing, then," Josh told her.

They got into line, and Josh accepted the bowl that was given him, but winced as an elderly woman dumped a ladle of brownish-gray gruel in it. Whatever warmth there was in the stuff was immediately canceled out by a second ladle of milk, thin and blue, which meant the cream was saved for other things. He was glad to see loaves of bread on the tables, however, and ate all he could manage, not knowing what lay ahead.

Soon after the meal was over, they started out. The whole community, as far as Josh could tell, was a hodgepodge of cabins and bunkhouses, of families and extended families, sometimes two or three elderly couples to a cottage, with all meals prepared in the cookhouse so as to save room in the cabins for sleeping quarters. A few of the old men—widowers, perhaps—lived with the young men out of necessity, someone told him. A bed in the village at all, Josh guessed, was a privilege.

The wagon bounced along the narrow rutted lane, low-lying branches scraping their faces from time to time. The slightest bump was a jolt to Josh, and he pressed his lips together to keep from groaning aloud. Some of the workers chatted among themselves, others settled back with arms folded, eyes closed, as even the ruts gave way to underbrush, and finally the wagon stopped.

They appeared to be on the shady side of a deep gully, among a mixed stand of maple, basswood, and elm. The ground was rocky, dense with undergrowth, and the diggers moved slowly, spreading out, some going one way, some another. Josh sensed for a time that Kaspar was following him, trying to work his way between Josh and the others, to separate him from the rest. So he stayed close to Mavis until finally Kaspar moved away.

Mavis noticed. "Don't cross Kaspar," she said. "He can get ugly."

"He *is* ugly," Josh responded. "Mean-ugly. And I'm not crossing him. He's *tailing* me. What's his problem?"

"He cannot accept," Mavis said simply.

"Accept what?"

She shrugged. "Everything. The fact that he's here."

"Well, I'd rather be somewhere else myself, but as long as I'm here, I intend to work," Josh said, hoping it would win him points. When she made no response, he turned his attention to the foliage around him. "Have you spotted any ginseng yet?"

"No, but that's not unusual," she told him. "That's why Old Sly sends so many of us out during digging season. He wants us to harvest all that's ready."

It was Mavis who helped Josh make his first and only find, and he felt like a real amateur when that was all he had in his pouch come noon. The wagon returned with a water barrel and tin cups, sausage, bread, and apples. The workers drank thirstily, then sat down on the side of the wagon, dangling their feet, or stretched out on the ground, eating lunch.

Josh had made up his mind that morning: he would leave before dinner. He would have worked one full day to pay for the food he'd had so far, and it would be better to leave before he accepted still more.

"I'm going to leave when we get back," he confided to Mavis. "There's enough daylight left that I can make a few miles, and it's mild weather. I'll sleep in the woods and hike some more tomorrow."

She looked thoughtful. "You'll be hungry," she said at last.

He showed her the bread in one hand, the

apple in the other. "I'll save this," he said. "It's enough to get me twenty miles or so."

She sighed and leaned back against the trunk of a tree, breaking off pieces of bread and popping them into her mouth.

Josh pushed at his gathering pouch with one foot. "If this stuff is so valuable, why don't you cultivate it? Plant the seeds in special beds and grow it by the ton?"

"Because it wouldn't be the same—not as potent. Cultivated ginseng even looks different. The traders can tell."

"Then why isn't everyone crowding up here to dig the wild stuff? You know—Gold Rush Appalachia or something?"

"No one knows it's here. Where we are, I mean. Maybe that's why it's been entrusted to us."

"By whom? Who owns this stuff? How did they hire you?"

She shrugged. "No one hires us. We own it. We always have."

"Gil said Chinese traders buy it. That you meet at The Edge, wherever that is. Who takes it to them?"

"Leone. She's my mother."

"Oh!" Josh studied her. "I *thought* you looked alike." He smiled at her.

"Isobel and Pardo go with her to do the negotiating," she told him.

"Isobel?"

"The oldest one in the village. Older than old. Twice in four seasons they go. It's from the traders we get the things we need—sugar, tools, shoes, salt. But if we have a special need, something they don't carry with them, we must place our order and wait till the next time to get it."

"You grew up here?"

"Yes, but not with Leone. My father's dead, and when Mother stopped speaking, the women raised me. It was her Sad Time."

"We both lost our fathers, then."

"It would seem so."

Josh wondered how much more he should ask. Not much, he decided, because Mavis rose suddenly and put her water jar back on the wagon. "I live with Eulaylia Goins now, Gil's mother. She and Daniel have been like parents to me. So Gil is almost my brother," she said. Then, slinging the strap of her pouch over her shoulder, she started off by herself, and Josh detected no signal for him to follow.

In the course of the afternoon, he found one more plant, but it was two-pronged, and he knew not to dig the roots. By the time the wagon came to fetch them again, he had only the one root that Mavis had helped him to find. Across the wagon, he could see Kaspar's eyes on his, trying to make contact. He looked the other way. The young man made him uneasy.

He rode silently back to the stable with the

others, and when he was paid for the plant he had dug—U.S. currency, he noticed—he put the money in his pack. Then he went immediately to the river to bathe. From the bank he got an occasional whiff of vegetables cooking, apples simmering. He wondered when they would miss him, if anyone would ask.

As he returned to the stable to pack up, he noticed a peach tree near the clearing, with wormy fruit. It would do, however. He had also seen berries in the woods. He'd survive.

He tied his sneakers, slipped the pack on his back, and stepped outside. The older folk were already heading for dinner, waiting for the bell to sound. Straight ahead, however, stood Kaspar and a group of young men from the bunkhouses.

They studied him cynically as he advanced, a smile playing on Kaspar's lips.

Josh knew, without thinking it through, that although he was feeling stronger, he wasn't this strong yet. He could take on one of them, perhaps, but he could not fight six or seven. Break another rib and he'd be here that much longer.

"Well," he said, trying to make a joke of it. "Maybe not."

He went back inside the stable, his heart pounding, and slipped off the pack. Now he knew what he had to do. Tell no one. He would pick the day carefully, and no one would see him go.

six

PERHAPS he could not trust any of them. Mavis must have told the others he was leaving. Embarrassed, he did not go to dinner when the bell sounded. The next time he chose to start out, it would be early morning, just before daybreak.

At breakfast the next morning, Josh expected ridicule when he reached the line that moved slowly into the cookhouse, but the diggers and other workers went sleepily from kettle to table and paid him little attention.

Gil slid in beside him on the bench. He was a likable fellow simply because he was polite. His eyes were brown and his skin olive-hued, with the same finely chiseled features as Josh himself. The boy asked with sincerity how Josh felt.

"I'm sorry they've put you up in the stable," he said. "When someone leaves, there will be a bed for you."

Josh felt heartened at this remark. People *did* leave, then. He smiled at the boy with the high forehead and bright eyes, like someone out of a nursery rhyme. Unlike the young men of twenty, he wore suspenders to hold up his muslin pants, a strange mix of modern and medieval, and his haircut had an Amish look, as though trimmed using the top of his head as the point of a compass. For the first time Josh noticed some younger children off to a table by themselves, beginning to be a little noisier and feistier than when they had first filed in to eat.

"When was the last time anyone left?" Josh asked.

"Last winter, I think. Someone died."

As encouraged as Josh had been before, he was dismayed now. "That's the only way out? To die?" he asked.

"What else?" Gil replied.

Josh tried to ignore his reply. "The night I came, someone mentioned Jack. Talked about digging his grave. Who was he?"

"Mavis's father, I think. Yes, I'm sure of it. Mavis Jack is her name, so he was her father."

"You take your father's first name for your last?"

"Sometimes. They call me Gil Daniel."

"When did Jack die?"

"Long ago."

"A year? Many years?"

Gil tipped his bowl so that all the milk left in it filled his spoon, and after he had cleaned the last drop, he said, "Time isn't the same here, Josh. That's what I learned in school. Here there is yesterday, today, and tomorrow. That and the seasons."

Josh leaned toward him until he almost forced the young boy to look directly into his eyes. "Where *is* this place, Gil? This village— does it have a name?"

"Canara, of course."

"Canara." Josh tried to recall his geography. "What state is it in?"

"I don't know. I'd tell you if I did. I've heard some say it's where Virginia meets the West. And, of course, it moves."

"*What?*"

"Yes. You go to bed at night with the hills on your left, and you wake up to find them on your right."

"Then *you* must have moved in the night; that's obvious."

"You'll see," Gil said simply.

Josh stared at him. "You *believe* this?"

"Of course!"

Josh sucked in his breath. "Who was the last person who came to Canara? Can you remember?"

"Kaspar," said Gil. "But I don't think he likes it much."

Little wonder, thought Josh, but aloud he said, "Why doesn't he leave then?"

"They say it's not easy, but I've never tried."

Inbreeding, Josh thought. *This is what happens—you pass the same defects down, generation to generation.* He wondered about Gil's parents. "Daniel's your father?"

"Yes. He's in charge of the sheep and pigs. I help him out when 'sang season's over."

The cookhouse bell rang, signaling the end of breakfast and the start of the day's work. The thing about the note it struck, Josh realized suddenly, was that it began as a distant ring and grew steadily louder, like a train whistle, until the blast was fast upon you. Then it stopped abruptly.

"Well, here's to your pouch!" Gil said enthusiastically. "If it can't come back full, may it not come back empty."

"Thank you," said Josh, and watched the boy go, thinking how little Gil knew of the world. But he couldn't help liking him, even if he was as wacky as they came.

When Josh walked back to the stable after breakfast, he passed Pardo, who was raking up black walnuts that lay strewn about the ground. The man stopped and smiled.

"It's helping, eh? The taping? You move easier."

"Yes. I have to be careful, but it helps a lot.

Thank you," Josh said, mindful that he might need the kindly man's help in the future. "I was wondering . . . can you tell me where we are, exactly? I mean, what state this village is in?"

"Ah!" Pardo smiled slightly and shook his head. "I never went to school."

Josh stared at him. "But you do know this is the United States, don't you?"

"Canara was here long before there were states," Pardo replied. That alone told Josh that Pardo knew a great deal more than he let on.

Nevertheless, Josh looked about, as though he were satisfied with the answer. "It's a nice day," he ventured. "I see you have pigs and chickens. Cows, too."

"Yes. We keep the cows for milk and cream."

"Dogs?" Josh asked casually. "I thought I heard dogs barking last night."

"Not here," said Pardo, returning to his task.

When he left the man, Josh vowed to recite to himself every state and its capital, to do the multiplication tables, and to write down any poem he'd ever learned and the words to every song he knew, so that he would not get caught up in this craziness. He would not allow his mind to go fallow. He needed every bit of intelligence he had so that when it came time to leave, he would have no doubt as to who he was or where he was headed.

Old Sly was harnessing the horses, and Josh found Mavis at the other end of the stable, patting the chestnut gelding, not the dappled mare that Leone had driven the night she found him. Mavis sang to it softly, and the horse twitched its ear.

"Well, are you happy now?" he challenged, and wished that his voice had not carried quite so much sarcasm.

She looked at him blankly. "I'm always happy. Why should I be happier now?"

"I'm still here," Josh told her, then reddened when he realized how self-important that must have sounded.

"I knew you would be," she said simply.

"So you tipped them off?"

"What are you talking about?" She took the brush she'd been using on the gelding's sleek coat and placed it on the shelf.

"Kaspar and the others. Blocking the road last night as I was about to leave."

She turned and gave him such a look of dismissal that Josh felt his face burn. "They had just loaded up a wagon with wood for Daniel to take around to the cookhouse and were talking there, waiting for dinner. I was over by the peach trees. I saw. What had that to do with you?"

Josh blushed deeper still. What a coward he must seem.

"I thought . . . I don't know. I was mistaken, I guess."

"If you want to go, Josh, go!" Mavis told him.

"I can leave anytime?"

"No one will stop you, least of all Kaspar."

Josh began to feel he was losing his mind. To keep himself focused he repeated his circumstances to himself: *I was hitchhiking to Dallas. I was mugged, and woke up here. I am probably in either Virginia or Tennessee, and I will get out!* He said no more to Mavis, but went to one of the privies—a primitive two-seater, surrounded by a privacy fence and roof—then returned and climbed aboard a wagon with the others for the long trek to the oak grove where each would do his solitary digging.

"Tomorrow's rest day, so today we dig double," Old Sly said, as if it could make any difference. What they found they found, Josh reasoned.

He was not surprised, when the diggers climbed down off the wagon and set out in different directions, that Kaspar went along with him. He was curious to know what the young man had to say, yet at the same time, he felt wary.

"*I* should be following *you*," Josh said, turning around to face him. "I certainly don't know where the ginseng is."

"Just keep walking. I want to talk," Kaspar said. It was more like an order, and Josh felt his temper rising.

As Kaspar moved closer, stepping sideways up the dark, steep incline, Josh said, "Someone told me the digging's over after the first frost, when the leaves and berries drop off."

Kaspar grunted. "For amateurs, maybe. I've worked it several seasons now. You get to know the plant, you can find it even then."

"How long have you been here?"

"Two years. Two long stinking years. And you're going to help me get out."

"*You*? What about me?"

"You're included."

"So what am I supposed to do?"

"How badly do you want out?"

"As much as you do."

"How far are you willing to go to escape?"

"What are you talking about?"

"You have to be willing to do *anything*."

"That depends," Josh said quickly as other diggers came in sight, and immediately swung himself down around a boulder and headed off in a different direction. He didn't trust Kaspar as far as he could walk without hurting his rib, which was not at all. He had nothing to go on but intuition at this point. He was inclined to trust no one, but if he had to choose, on a scale of one to ten, Mavis would get an eight and Kaspar a zero.

Again, it was a futile search—he found no ginseng. *What did it matter?* Josh thought. If tomorrow was a rest day, he would rise early and follow the road out. He would leave the whole bedeviled woods to Kaspar.

He gave himself the pleasure of riding back beside Mavis on the wagon, shoes in hand, their bare feet dangling over the side to cool them, and was glad that she seemed no longer irritated with him, as she had been that morning. Their bodies were warm from the day's work, and Mavis's sweat gave off a sweetish odor. She sang softly as they bumped along, and Old Sly smiled.

"Little songbird," he said affectionately from the back of the wagon. "It's what your name means, you know."

For only a millisecond, Josh imagined himself living here for the rest of his life—this compared with being a lonely nobody down in Dallas. He shook his head suddenly to rid it of the thought. Was he crazy?

Mavis began talking excitedly about what she would do on their rest day. The older workers spoke of personal chores that needed doing—clothes to be washed and dried in the sun, harnesses to mend—but the younger girls talked of going to The Stop. Most of the women were smaller and darker than Mavis, their hands and feet petite and well-shaped, despite the physical work.

"The moon's full," said a pretty girl named

Sylvania whom Josh had noticed before. "Let's walk over tomorrow evening—make a night of it."

"You want to go, Kaspar?" Gil called.

The young man with the deep scowl shrugged. "Perhaps."

You'll go without me, Josh thought. *By tomorrow, I'll be long gone.*

He was careful to follow the usual routine when they reached the village. He washed his face at the pump, ate heartily in the cookhouse and, once again, managed to slip several pieces of bread and some cheese in a pocket before he left the table.

Later, at the river, he laid his clothes on the bank with the men and boys and plunged into the cold water, sucking in his breath as his body shriveled, trying not to loosen the thin straps of cloth that bound his chest. How could it be August, he wondered, and the river so cold? Perhaps they were even higher up in the mountains than he had thought.

As they passed the lye soap from one to another, Old Sly edged toward Josh. "Kaspar brought in a large pouch again today," he said.

Josh shrugged. "I didn't notice."

"He's not to be trusted," Old Sly went on. "Are you?"

Josh gave no answer. The man wouldn't believe him anyway. Why not just let them go? He remembered what Mavis had told him—that no one kept them here; they were free to leave whenever they liked. If that was true, why was Kaspar still here?

Josh made ready that evening to leave at dawn, gathering up the clothes he had strewn about the hay. He had just opened his pack to put them in when Mavis came through the doorway, and so, instead of packing them up, Josh made as though he were sorting his stuff.

"When you have a proper bed, there'll be a place for your things," she told him.

"It's okay. I like the stable."

"It's cold in winter. You won't like it then."

"How soon will someone be leaving—so that I can have a bed?"

"Who can tell? We always lose some in winter."

Josh had already decided he would get into no more mind games with anyone. They all had the knack of turning your words back onto themselves. Then he realized Mavis was referring to death, and changed the subject. "Do you get a rest day often?"

"In 'sang season. At harvest there's little rest at all, for the hay must be brought in when it's dry and the women have their fill of work in the cookhouse." She studied him. "What about you? What will you do tomorrow?"

"Sleep late, for one thing," Josh joked, taking out the shirt he had stuffed in only a moment before. "Wash my socks, maybe."

"You'll never sleep late here." Mavis laughed. "The roosters see to that."

"Then I'll turn in early. I'm tired," he told her.

"Sleep well," she said.

Josh slept hard at first, more fitfully after that, afraid he would sleep past dawn. He did fall into a deep slumber an hour before light, but at the first crow of a cock, he was instantly awake.

The stable had the same gray cast, but of a lighter shade, and he guessed it was just after five. In a matter of minutes he had thrust his remaining garments and possessions into his pack, searched with his fingers through the burlap bedding to see if he had forgotten anything, then gone stealthily to the rain barrel and, after a long drink, followed the wagon ruts in the lane up the hill away from the village, the clay underfoot blood red in the breaking light.

Canara appeared to be sleeping, but still Josh was uneasy. A thin stream of blue smoke rose from the chimney of the cookhouse, so the cooks, at least, were awake. When Josh came to the first bend in the lane, he half expected to see Kaspar and the other young men waiting as before. But there were only trees around the bend, and the next and the next. As he walked on, the sun warmed his head, and Josh felt a great lifting of spirits, and even smiled to himself at the ease with which he had left Canara behind.

They were undoubtedly the oddest people he had ever met, and he could only guess that the long years of isolation had affected them all. He was glad to have done with them, though he'd liked Mavis and Gil. Pardo, too.

Overhead, several large birds were circling, drifting with the air currents on their widespread wings. Josh felt he didn't much care if it took him one day or three to reach the interstate; he'd make it. He could ration out the cheese and bread, eat mountain apples along the way, and fill his flask from the many springs that flowed from the hills. Once he reached the freeway, he would stick to it. No more detours for him.

He regretted very much the theft of his watch, for now he had only the sun and shadows to tell him how time was progressing, and when he guessed it to be about seven, he sat down and allotted himself a fourth of the bread and cheese. He *would* have a story to tell when he started a new school down in Texas.

When he had rested and drunk as much water as he felt his stomach would hold, he laboriously lifted the backpack to his shoulders once more and set off, trying to ignore the pain in his rib. Overhead the birds were still circling, and Josh guessed they were either hawks enjoying the summer breeze or buzzards looking for carrion.

Every time he went over a rise or around a bend, he expected to see a distant water tower, a plane; smokestacks from a faraway factory, perhaps; the gleam of a roof or silo. But every time he was disappointed, for over each hill and around each bend there was nothing but more trees, so that finally he began to be bored with disappointment and expected nothing. He remembered how long the man who mugged him had driven about. He was obviously expecting the interstate far too soon. Josh was faithfully following the wagon wheel ruts, and that was enough.

There was a brief shower, and he sank down on a rock to rest, taking off his shoes awhile, not even caring that his shirt was soaked. But the rain soon stopped, the sun came out again, and Josh put his sneakers back on, wishing he still had the Nikes that had been stolen.

He rubbed his shoulder where the straps of his backpack had left the skin feeling raw, then started off again. He was tired, however, and things began looking the same to him—the hills, the road, the mud. At last he sensed an opening in the trees ahead, and could hear the steady sound of a shovel hitting the ground and striking rock, someone clearing a field, perhaps.

He was certain he was close to human habitation, if only a hermit far out in the woods. He would offer to work for a meal. A few directions, and he'd be off again in an hour or two.

Hurrying on a little faster and ignoring the rawness of his shoulder, Josh went over the last rise and around the bend. He stopped, his breath coming fast, his strength giving way. There below was Canara, yellow in the morning sun, and Pardo, clearing a patch of ground.

seven

HOW could this be?

Josh stared at the figures moving around in the sunlight—mothers taking their children down to the river to bathe, the curl of smoke above the cookhouse, Old Sly drawing water at the well. There was that strange, but now familiar, awareness again, like something invisible surrounding the place. The ginseng, maybe? Or something more, too hard to describe.

He could understand that he might have taken a wrong turn and circled back to Canara, except that he was positive there had been no fork in the road, not a single place he'd had to decide, *this way or that?*

Most puzzling of all was the fact that he was not entering the village by another route, but was coming back the very same way he had gone. Like the birds overhead, like the ripples in the rain barrel, he had come back upon himself without ever meeting the road on which he had started out. It was as if a straight road led to two places. Perhaps, as Gil said, the hills did move. He had completely lost his bearings.

The only explanation he could think of was that there might be another road out of the village. He had been totally out of his head the night Leone had brought him here; he had no idea from what direction they had come, only that the wagon was there in the stable when he awoke. He would have to put his things back again, and he churned with frustration as he came down the hill. Only Pardo looked his way and stopped, resting one arm on his shovel.

"And so," he said, "you went nowhere."

Josh studied the man before answering— the coarsely woven tunic over his baggy trousers, the collarless shirt, like something out of the sixteenth century.

"I figured I'd been a burden long enough," he ventured. "You've all been very kind. But I've got an aunt who needs me, so I thought I'd hike back to the interstate. It seems I took the wrong road."

Pardo's dark blue eyes fixed themselves on him.

"No, lad, there is no wrong road. You took the only road we have."

"Then I missed the fork somehow. I followed the wagon tracks, and they brought me back here again. I didn't see any turnoff."

Pardo nodded. "The ruts go there and back," he said. It was the type of cryptic remark that was driving Josh mad.

"Look. Leone picked me up out on a road somewhere the night she brought me here. There's obviously a way out. You can't keep me prisoner. Someone will call the police if I don't show."

Pardo put out his hand and gently touched Josh's arm as if to calm him. "Joshua, there are no gates, no locks, no walls. We keep no prisoners. You may wander as you will. Truly, if I knew the way out of Canara, I would tell you—Kaspar, too. But I don't. If there is a way, you must find it yourself." He picked up his shovel again and, with a nod, continued his work.

Like a cold wind sweeping in from the pass, a feeling of profound dread crept over Josh's body, causing gooseflesh on his arms. The man had been brainwashed! They'd all been brainwashed into thinking there was no way out. Slaves, that's what they were. Someone had thought up this scheme to get ginseng diggers. If Chinese traders dealt with Pardo and Leone, they came from somewhere. They met somewhere. Traders didn't just crawl up out of the ground!

More and more, Josh's thoughts turned

toward his aunt in Texas. She surely would have missed him by now, and— He stopped in his tracks as a second cold wind raked its fingers over him. She would not miss him until the twenty-fourth of August, when his plane was due. She thought he was backpacking with friends along the Appalachian Trail.

He was following the Appalachian Trail, all right, he thought ruefully as he dropped his pack down in the stable; he'd followed it here to no-man's-land, among a bunch of people with defective genes, that's what. The villagers of Canara were probably so browbeaten by Old Sly or whomever that they couldn't find their way out of a paper bag.

Most maddening of all, he, Josh himself, was losing track of time. His watch was gone. There were no clocks in Canara. No calendar, even. There was only the rising of the sun and the clang of the dinner bell to mark the day. It would have been August back in Massachusetts, but here it felt like September. October, even.

Although it had seemed to him that he had been up and walking for hours that morning, the villagers were just now heading to the cook-house for breakfast, and he heard the clang of the bell once again. He felt too frustrated to eat, and dreaded making conversation with anyone, but it seemed important that he appear to be settling in. Resigned, at least. And so he followed the others down the path and stood in the breakfast line, awaiting his plate and cup.

For a rest day, no one seemed to be resting. In the clearing, two women were standing over a huge iron kettle in which bubbled and boiled the most foul-smelling mixture Josh had come across in a long time. With sleeves rolled up, they each had hold of a heavy stick—more like a pole—that they clasped with both hands, and stirred the stuff round and round. Josh recognized the smell of the soap he was given at the river.

Moving slowly up the breakfast line, he observed the residents of Canara. They didn't seem unhappy to him—nor particularly animated, either, but then it was early. The younger children were too sleepy at this hour to make much noise, and stood resting their heads against their parents' hands until they were given their corn bread and gruel.

Farm animals, Josh thought in despair. We're like workhorses, glad for a day of rest when we can graze. If he ever made it out of here . . .

Again the quick rush of wind, only this time he recognized it for what it was: fear.

When he made it out of here, he corrected himself, he would alert the state police, the newspapers . . . They'd have helicopters flying overhead, and people would wonder how it was possible that a group of people could have been tricked into forced labor for so many generations. This adventure was far more than he'd bargained for, and he tried to imagine the pleasure he'd have in relating all this to his new friends in Dallas. But beneath the bravado, his heart kept up a steady drumbeat of apprehension.

He looked around for Mavis, but she wasn't in the dining hall—the young men and women, it seemed, were sleeping late, for now and then one straggled in, face still puffy.

Josh slid onto the bench beside Eulaylia.

"Good morning," she said genially.

"Good morning. Gil still sleeping?" he asked.

The sturdy woman returned his smile. "He likes to sleep more than he likes to eat. On rest day, he's always the last one to the cookhouse."

"I'm still trying to get acquainted with everyone," Josh explained.

"It takes a while," she answered.

After a few pleasantries about the weather, Josh decided to risk it, and asked Eulaylia about Leone. If there were other mute people in the village, he thought—surely an oddity, since she could hear perfectly well—he would be convinced more than ever that inbreeding had dulled both their speech and their minds.

"I've noticed," he said, "that Leone never speaks."

"Yes," Eulaylia replied, sticking her knife in the crock of white butter on the table and slathering it on her bread. "But years ago she spoke, before Mavis was born."

"Something happened in childbirth, then?"

"No. Before then. We don't speak of it much, Joshua. It was her great tragedy, and she has not said a word since that day. She's gaumy."

"Disturbed?"

"No, sad."

The word awakened some long-ago memory in him. His grandfather—his father's father—had used that word sometimes when he was tired. But he focused on the subject of Leone again. Mavis was at least sixteen, he figured. Seventeen, he guessed. If Leone had stopped speaking even before then . . .

"And after she was born, Mavis came to live with you? Because Leone had stopped speaking?"

"Yes."

"And for seventeen, eighteen years Leone's been silent? Has she seen a doctor?"

"We are our own doctors in Canara," Eulaylia said. "This is a place of healing. For some it just takes longer than for others."

Fools! Josh thought, and stuffed a piece of bread in his mouth, more to keep from saying the wrong thing than to feed hunger. But finally, when he sensed that Eulaylia was finished and about to leave, he asked, "Is it impolite to ask what the tragedy was? I won't speak of it to Leone, of course."

Eulaylia lowered her voice. "She lost her young man."

"Her husband?"

"Her lover."

"Oh. I'm sorry," Josh said. "Mavis is all she has, then, even though they don't live together?"

"Isobel, the Old One, took Leone in, at the time of her sadness. She's lived there ever since, and will, of course, forever." Eulaylia gathered her utensils and plate and, with a nod to Josh, left the table.

Actually, Josh didn't see that he'd learned much of anything helpful. The only thing that was clear to him was that somehow the way out of Canara was kept a mystery. No one blocked his path, it was true. As Pardo said, there were no locks, no walls. Josh had just come back, that's all. His feet had returned to the starting point, and he couldn't seem to get beyond that.

After he had eaten, he strolled about. Everyone seemed to be busy at some chore or other on their rest day. The difference, as far as he could tell, was that no one worked very hard at it. The young children who were gritting corn, for example—scraping ears of field corn on an old piece of tin with nail holes punched in it—would lay down their scrapers every now and then to chase after a hen that had wandered by, or to wade awhile in the river.

The women who were making the smelly soap laughed at a shared joke as they worked, and occasionally one or the other would go over to sit in the shade, unbuttoning her shirt and fanning herself. The young men who had been chopping wood at the back of the cookhouse stopped to heave a small block of particularly smooth wood at one another like a football. The game continued for several minutes as Josh watched—each man having to guess whether the "ball" would be passed to him next or to someone else, and having to react quickly when the wooden missile came his way. One tall young man misjudged the pass and the wood hit him squarely on the shoulder, to the merriment of the others. If any were unhappy here, Kaspar excepted, they didn't show it. Josh almost wished he had brought a real football along just to teach them the game.

No! he suddenly told himself, and was horrified to discover he was thinking about what he would do were he to stay, were he to be trapped here. No! He would not allow even the thought. *I will leave!* he whispered under his breath, determined to repeat it every day like a mantra. *It might not be tomorrow, but I'll explore every inch of the place till I find the road out. The next time Leone goes to meet the traders, I'll follow.*

With no job assigned to him, Josh set off around the perimeter of the clearing, searching for every sign of a path leading off into the woods—any evidence of wagon wheel ruts. He discovered that the villagers did not keep their hogs penned, but let them run in the woods, feeding on the mast that the forest produced— the chestnuts, acorns, and beechnuts that were beginning to fall from the trees, and for which pigs rooted now, searching for early bounty. The weather here in this mountain country was getting the look of autumn already, and despite the sun, a chill breeze blew in now and then, which foretold the distant arrival of winter.

Josh made a full circle of the clearing. He saw hay fields and rows of corn, a vegetable garden and orchard, but nothing that looked like a road except for one overgrown path that led who knew where. It was not wide enough to permit a wagon, and Josh could tell from the undergrowth that no wheels had come this way for a very long time.

As he stood there pondering, however, he heard once again the far-off barking and snarling of dogs. *Wagon or no wagon,* he thought, *that's the way I'll go.* But not today. He'd explore a bit first, plan his escape. Next time, when he got his chance, he wanted to do it right.

He was heading back toward the well for a drink when he saw Leone pushing a small cart of what looked to be old rags. Then the bundle moved, and a long thin hand reached out and gestured. Leone leaned down to readjust the blanket and pat the hand, and it disappeared once again.

"Good morning," Josh said, and went on his way, adding to his list of rules the fact that one did not mention Leone's long-ago lover and the way Isobel had taken Leone in. Now, he noticed, Leone cared for the old woman.

When he saw Mavis that afternoon, she was feeding a crow that had become a pet, and he sauntered over, bemused. The crow was standing on the railing at the far end of the fence while Mavis held a piece of bread in her outstretched hand. The crow studied the hand and the bread sideways and moved about from one foot to the other, then tipped back its head and cawed. Other crows answered, flying in from tree to tree, until dark bundles of birds hovered in the branches overhead.

Cockily, hesitantly, the crow did his strut-walk down the fence rail, stopping now and then with one foot raised to survey the situation, till at last it reached the outstretched hand. The head darted forward, the beak snatched up the bread, and the crow flew skyward.

"If he's smart, he'll circle back and share that with the others," Mavis mused. "It wouldn't pay to just fly off."

"How long did it take you to teach him that?" Josh asked, watching the crows watch them.

"Several seasons," she said. "Midnight, we call him. Crows are wary, but he's the tamest of them all. Are you enjoying your rest day?"

"Not much," Josh answered truthfully. "I don't really feel at home here."

"You will," she said. "Everyone does eventually." And then—in almost a whisper—she corrected herself. "Except my father. He didn't."

"Oh?" Josh noticed the way Mavis turned her head away. "Whatever happened to him, I'm sorry," he said.

Mavis gave him a good look. "I suppose you've heard the gossip."

"About what? I haven't been here long enough to learn the rules, much less the gossip."

She turned away again and stared up at the sky, where all the crows were flying now, Midnight still in the lead, a dim speck against the clouds. "Well, you will. The worst sort of gossip, too."

"Then I won't listen."

That seemed to soothe her, but Mavis searched his face as she spoke. "Oh, yes you will. A story has nowhere else to go here but around, and each time it circles, someone adds a little something. All my father ever wanted was to leave."

"Is that a crime?"

"It would seem so."

Josh slowly shook his head. "This is a strange place," he mused.

"Strange to you, perhaps, but I was born here," Mavis said. "It's all I know."

There was a commotion in the sky and Josh and Mavis looked up to see a whirlwind of crows against the clouds.

Mavis sucked in her breath. "He wasn't ready," she said. "He shouldn't have gone."

Josh wasn't sure whether she was talking about her father or her crow, but the huge flock of birds was circling rapidly now, faster and faster, a vortex of black that suddenly spiraled downward like a dagger, and a moment later a crow lay dead at their feet.

It was Midnight.

eight

AS the shadows of afternoon lengthened, the young men and women began to talk about The Stop, anticipating their evening out. When Mavis asked Josh whether or not he was going— whether he would *like* to go—Josh said yes. If only to explore the settlement, he decided. Look for clues, lay his plans.

The whole mood of Canara seemed to change, as though, for this one night, youth was in charge. Instead of eating the evening meal first and bathing afterward, the young people went to the pump and the river early and came to the table wearing fresh shirts. Some of the girls, Josh noticed, had exchanged their muslin trousers for dresses, long and homespun look- ing, of unbleached cotton. Mavis had fastened her hair up in back with a comb, and the old folk of the village smiled at the girls admiringly, encouragingly, as they came to dinner.

There was much joking and laughing at the tables. But the burly young men in collarless shirts and the young women with petal-stained lips—who, Josh noticed, often pinched their cheeks to make them pink—left as soon as they had eaten. They stopped off at the stable for lanterns, then set out merrily across the cornfield in the gathering darkness. Even Kaspar was part of the crowd, but Josh avoided him.

The younger boys—Gil's age—leaped and frolicked along the edge of the moving crowd, being silly, yet not too silly, for it was clear that they had only recently been inducted into the company of the older ones. Those closer to Josh's age sauntered lazily along, teasing, jostling, whispering, laughing, some of them pairing off with girls, hands clasped. The girl named Sylvania cast amused glances at Josh from time to time, tossing her hair, then making a playful clicking sound with her tongue when he looked back at her. That little gesture reminded Josh again of his paternal grandfather—the way he used to click his tongue when he was teasing. Strange how being here in Canara brought back memories of long ago.

Mavis, who had been walking with the other girls, hung back after a time, until Josh caught up with her. He was purposely staying to the rear so that his eyes could take in as much as possible while there was any light at all. He had been around the same field they were in earlier in the day, and had seen no evidence of a path. But when they reached the rail fence at the far end, the tall young man in the lead climbed on top and helped each girl in turn step over into the blackness of the trees beyond.

For a while Josh could see nothing but the lights from the swinging lanterns, and the woods had an eerie glow, as though lit by luminous dancing sprites.

"I notice you have an admirer," Mavis teased.

"The dark-eyed girl?"

"Sylvania, yes."

"I'm not much in the mood for romance," he told her.

"That's good, because she's soon getting married."

"To whom?"

"One of the fellows. Tom."

"Then why is she flirting with me?"

"She won't, after she's married. This is her last big night of freedom. Tom would do the same. It's all in fun."

In a way, Josh was sorry.

"I'm glad you decided to come," Mavis told him. "You were getting too serious."

"I just lost my mother, Mavis."

"Oh, I am so thoughtless! I'm sorry," she apologized, looking genuinely chagrined.

"But besides that, I never know when you're kidding or not," he told her. "Finding myself stuck a thousand miles from where I'm supposed to be—that's not serious?"

"I didn't mean that. It's just that you act as though you have to figure everything out right this minute."

"By August twenty-fourth, to be exact. My airline ticket."

"Well, anyway, I hope you enjoy tonight."

He tried to be more genial, not ruin it for her. "I'm going to try. What's The Stop? The local hangout?"

His expressions sometimes threw her, he could tell, so he tried again. "Where your crowd goes on rest days?"

"Only when it comes round again."

"Your rest day?"

"No. The Stop. When the time is right."

"Why? What would happen if you went and it wasn't the right time?"

"It wouldn't be there!"

"You mean it comes and goes? It disappears? Why does everyone talk in riddles?" Josh couldn't help feeling annoyed.

Mavis looked uncomfortable, as though being asked to explain a physics problem she didn't understand. "I don't *know* any of that, Josh! Can't you just enjoy it, like everyone else?"

Josh knew if he lost Mavis as an ally, he'd

lose his best hope. "Okay," he said. "Where else do you go on rest days? What else do you and your friends do?"

"Well, sometimes we swim at night."

"Ever swim all the way across?"

"No. We never do that."

"Why not?"

She looked exasperated again, so Josh apologized quickly. "I'm sorry. I'm not used to living in a cage."

"Now *you* talk in riddles!" She laughed. "Let's hurry and catch up with the others. I am going to dance until my feet drop off."

The path in the woods ascended so steeply that at first they seemed to be crawling, their hands grasping at any protruding rock or root. Mavis held her skirt bunched before her so she wouldn't trip, but as soon as she reached the top of the hill, she dropped it and stood holding her lantern to light Josh's way.

He moved up beside her and exclaimed as he looked down at a roadside restaurant in the clearing below, then laughed with relief. The windows were lit, and the first thought in his head was to find a telephone. He rummaged quickly in his pocket, and was delighted when his fingers closed around a quarter. He'd get the operator, ask to reverse the charges . . .

As they went down the bank on the other side and drew closer, however, he realized that there was no electricity; those who had arrived first had set their lanterns in the windows, and once again he felt the sharp sting of disappointment. Going up the cracked sidewalk thatched with weeds, he could see an old green and white sign dangling askew from one corner of the low wood building. THE STOP, it said, with the faded caricature of a steam engine on it.

Still, Josh thought, roadside restaurants sometimes sprang up in old abandoned depots where trains once ran. And if trains did run once, no matter how long ago, might there not be some old rails in place, railroad ties rotting in the track bed? All he would have to do if he found them would be to follow along and they would take him somewhere.

Mavis was tugging at his arm, pulling him inside, and Josh was startled to hear music— first one instrument, then another and another—until the warming up became a tune, and suddenly the floor in front of him was filled with whirling couples in a strange dance he could not quite recognize. The closest he could come to describing it was a square dance, but the young people were moving in time to dulcimers, not fiddles, and from time to time the dancing became a line, not a square. It was the kind of music he imagined Mideast bluegrass might be, if there was such a thing.

He didn't know what he was doing, and his

feet were even more confused, but he found himself being passed from one young woman to another, one smiling face blending into the next and the next. Sylvania locked her hands around the back of his neck as they danced and talked to him with her eyes. The flashes of face, the flickering lanterns, and the whirling made him fairly dizzy. When the first set ended at last and some of the dancers traded places with musicians to give them a chance on the floor, Josh begged off and went over to sit on one of the dusty chairs by the paint-peeling tables, trying to get his bearings.

At what once had been a bar, some of the young men were filling mugs with a golden brown liquid from a large cask they had brought along. Josh walked over to taste some and found it to be hard cider. Holding his mug in both hands, he wandered around the edge of the room while the dancers twisted and whirled to a new tune.

There was a large blackboard by the doorway to the kitchen, the chalk notations so faded that Josh could scarcely read them. Two of the entrees were legible, however—BISCUITS AND SAUSAGE GRAVY and CORN BREAD AND SOUP. One thing was for sure; this wasn't New York City.

He went to the jukebox in the corner—dusty, broken, tilting slightly to the left. There must have been electricity once, he thought.

Songs he didn't recognize: "High Cotton," "She Drives Me Crazy," "Buck Naked," "Cherry Pie," "Paradise City" . . .

Farther on, in a dirty glass case off to one side, Josh saw items that convinced him that although this might have started as a train depot, it had since become a truck stop, though he had seen no sign of a highway. There were diesel fuse holders, CB parts, booster cables, power cords . . . The reason no one had taken them, Josh decided, was that the people of Canara didn't even know what they were.

When the third set of music and dancing started up, the first musicians leaving the dance floor to take up their dulcimers again, Josh was afraid that if he stuck around he'd be drafted once more, and was relieved when the dancing began without him. It occurred to him that this might be the time to slip outside and locate the train tracks or the remnants of a road, if there were any. He might be noticed if he tried to make his way through the smiling dancers to get to the front door, so he moved toward the kitchen and, when no one seemed to be looking, pushed open the swinging doors and slipped inside.

Instantly he felt two strong hands around his throat, the hard cider smell on someone's breath in his face.

Sylvania's betrothed. It was all he could figure.

Josh grabbed at the hands, forcing the fingers away from his windpipe, but he was backed against a wall, and in the faint light coming through the windows of the swinging doors, Josh saw that he was looking into the face of Kaspar.

He let go with his right hand and punched a fist into the young man's stomach, sending Kaspar reeling backward a step or two. Cement. That's what the abdomen felt like. The guy had abs like a washboard.

"You crazy?" Josh gasped, fists clenched, ready to take him on. His rib, however, ached with the exertion. "What's with you, anyway?"

Kaspar glared at him in the semidarkness. They were both breathing heavily.

"As though I didn't have trouble enough!" Josh told him. "What's *your* problem?"

Kaspar may have had no inclination to continue the fight, but his mood was still surly. "You're going to help me get out of here," he said, sounding half drunk.

"Well, you sure have a strange way of asking."

"I'm not asking, I'm telling."

"If I knew how I got here, I'd be gone by now."

"You're the last one to come in. You must have seen something."

"It was night! One minute I'm lying on the road, and the next I'm in the stable and you're talking about killing me."

"Oh, you'll settle in like the others," Kaspar said thickly. "You'll just give up and let it happen. Mavis likes you; I see that already. You'll take orders from Old Sly, marry his granddaughter, and get to thinking you're one of them. This might be my last chance to leave."

"*What's* your last chance? Me? Now I know you're raving."

"I'm telling you this, Josh—you don't go in on this with me, I'll kill you. I swear it. Don't fall for Mavis. Don't fall for anybody or anything they tell you. You take your orders from me."

"Wrong." Josh felt his own temper rising. "I make my own orders. Order number one: get myself out. If you come along or not, that's your business." Josh leaned against the wall in the darkness, arms folded over his chest. "So what's your story, Kaspar? How did you get here?"

Kaspar drew in his breath and, as though to mimic Josh's stance, folded his arms and leaned against the broken-down refrigerator.

"Tristate rappelling championship. That's what I was practicing for. Penn State. Coach took us in the mountains during spring break— some place we'd never been. We were supposed to go off in twos, but my partner and I . . . we had different ideas about where we wanted to drop." Here Kaspar's voice took on an odd tone of incredulity and despair. "Once I got down into the valley, I couldn't get back up."

"Why? The rope gave? You lost your hold?"

"No . . . I just . . . I climbed and climbed . . . and got no closer to the top. I tried for two days, sure they'd come looking for me. You know—that the whole Penn State team would be here looking—helicopters, searchlights. Nothing. I haven't even seen a plane. No planes at all, as though even this piece of sky is over some alien world." Anger again. "Where the hell could they be, just to let me slip off the edge of the earth like that? Unless . . ." His voice trailed off. ". . . unless I wandered away so far that they searched in all the wrong places."

"What state are we in? I don't even know that."

Kaspar shrugged. "I've wished a thousand times I'd paid attention. I just picked up my bag and got in the van. Slept most of the way, if I remember. West Virginia. Tennessee. I don't know. But I'll do whatever it takes to get out of here. I am not living the rest of my life in Canara!"

"So what do you think the deal is? Why *can't* we get out?"

"We're Melungeon, they tell me."

"We're what?"

The kitchen doors swung open and Mavis came in.

"*Here* you are! We were all wondering! Come on out and be sociable." She grabbed both their arms at once and pulled them through the swinging doors. Her grip was strong, and Josh got the idea that no one, not even Kaspar, refused Mavis.

Within moments, it seemed, he was caught up again by the music of the hammered dulcimer, as rhythmical and haunting a beat as he had ever heard. The girlish faces flashed past him once again as bodies whirled. Men's boots were pounding the floor, women's hands were clapping, dresses spinning, hair flying, arms flinging . . . and then . . . almost as soon as the evening had begun, it was over.

What was the signal? Josh wondered. When did they know it was time? Like locusts, their chirping had all started and stopped together. Then the procession was making its way through the trees again, lanterns even brighter now because of the dark. From time to time couples slipped off into the trees, to emerge minutes later, arms around each other, reluctant, it seemed, to return.

Josh had no steady girl back home, but it made him miss the girls that he knew—their laughter, the fit of their jeans, their teasing, their hair . . . His junior year would have been so great—Karen Shroeder had started calling him sometimes—just to talk, she said. She liked him, he knew. They'd had plans. And then . . . his life was upside down, inside out.

He swallowed. Oh, God, he missed his mom. He'd never thought about losing her, never dreamed the pain could be so acute. He missed the smallest things about her! The little wrinkle near her mouth when she laughed, the scent of her shampoo . . . He couldn't picture his future without her. How could he get away when he didn't know where he was going? How could he know where he was going when he couldn't tell where he'd been? It was like a bad dream that never ended. He could see how the comfort of a girl's arms right now would help—and it was exactly what Kaspar had warned him against.

Well, Kaspar needn't worry. Mavis was too old for him, for one thing. And she was an Amazon of a girl. She might be interested in him, but not in the way Kaspar suspected. You could just tell things like that. Sylvania was a different matter, but she was already taken. And a girl named Imelda, with dark hair and even darker eyes . . . Josh felt a terrible longing. Not just for girls, but for home. For Mom. For everything.

He hated Kaspar, but the warning still rang in his ears. *Don't get involved; get out.* Well, he would if he could. He would come back here on his own and look for railroad tracks, for signs of a road, but he still felt that the answer lay in the direction of the barking he had heard. The dogs. And the first chance he got, he'd check it out.

nine

HE avoided Kaspar the next day. In one sense he was eager to find out what the guy knew about Canara and by what means he had tried to get out. But in another, he felt that being in cahoots with him on any level meant disaster. And so Josh went in Mavis's direction when they dug for ginseng, and sat with her when Leone returned in the wagon with their lunch at noon.

"It's a hot day," Mavis said, choosing the bank of a mountain stream on which to sit while she ate her bread and cheese, bare feet dangling in the water. "We don't have many of them here, and I'm glad when they're over." There was a faint line of perspiration above her upper lip, and she opened the neck of her shirt to cool herself.

Josh said, "Sometimes when I'm outside I feel this . . . sensation. I don't know. Other times I think it's a scent. As though the air around us is charged. Do you feel that, Mavis?"

"No," she answered.

"Is it summer or fall?"

"The autumn equinox is coming," she said. "I'm not sure exactly when."

"Then it's September already?"

"September? Is that one of your seasons? We go by moons, and only the old keep track of them."

Josh wished he could talk to her straight out, but he rarely got intelligible answers when he tried, and besides, whom could he believe? Not Kaspar, surely. Nor Old Sly. Gil seemed honest, but naive. The girl named Imelda was never serious for a moment, Sylvania too flirtatious . . . Pardo, perhaps? Josh wondered if he had resisted asking questions of Pardo because he was afraid of the answers.

"You are a long ways away, Josh," Mavis said after a moment, pulling out one foot and drying it on the hem of her tunic. "What are you thinking?"

Josh managed a smile. "I'm thinking about you."

She laughed. "That won't take long."

"Among other things, I'm wondering if you go to school."

"Yes. The younger children meet in the cookhouse each day for a lesson, but the rest of us will go regularly again after the harvest season. Eulaylia teaches and one of the men—

sometimes Pardo, sometimes Daniel. I don't like school much."

"Why not?"

"We learn what we already know—what we've heard before. The plants, the berries, what mushrooms you can eat, which ones you can't."

"What about literature, history, math, geography?"

"Those, too. Isobel has some books about the explorers, the continents and oceans. In mathematics we're very basic. If a cook has forty pounds of flour to feed two hundred and seventy-three people, and one pound of flour will feed five, how many pounds will he need if . . . that sort of thing." She laughed again, and it was the one thing that gave Josh hope—Mavis's laughter. The fact that she could live here and still laugh. "I like history best," she added, "but it's only *our* history. We are too closed inside ourselves. Again and again we circle back. And yet . . ." She frowned. "It's necessary."

Josh studied the girl. "What do they teach you about your own history?"

"Who we are. Where we came from."

He was interested. "Then you can be *my* teacher. How *did* you get here? I thought you were born here."

"I mean way, way back—where the Melungeons came from."

That word again. "The who?"

"Melungeons. That's who we are. You, too."

"Not me," Josh told her. "I'm Scotch-Irish."

Her eyes danced. "Vardy? That's Irish?"

He shrugged. "Well, that's what I always thought."

"We were studying names last unit. Many of the Melungeons came from Portugal, and the names changed over time. As soon as I saw you—your dark hair, dusky skin, blue eyes—and heard your name, I knew you were Melungeon."

"How?"

"Vardy is from Navarro. You're as Portuguese as Sylvania and Alonso and Elvas and Helena. I'm half Portuguese, half Celt. That's what my grandfather tells me. And there are still people in Canara who speak only Portuguese, who have passed it on down all these hundreds of seasons."

"What does Portugal have to do with anything?"

"It's where the Melungeons started. Some of us, anyway. In truth, I guess, we come from everywhere. The English at Jamestown were not the first European colony in America—we were. I know that much of history."

Josh could not help showing his skepticism. "Mavis, tell me this: People here marry and have children, right? And they . . . well, you all marry each other? Cousins marry cousins? I mean, maybe even brothers and sisters?"

She got to her feet suddenly and, with as angry a look as Josh had seen, reached for her boots and jerkily pulled them on.

"What kind of question is that?"

He tried to salvage the situation. "Look, I'm just trying to understand you. This place. How can I learn if I don't ask questions? Half the time I don't even get answers that make any sense."

She softened then. "I'm sorry."

Old Sly was clapping his hands, calling the workers back to their digging. Mavis wiped her forehead with her arm, then pushed both sleeves up above her elbows. "Someday soon, Josh, when there is time, I will tell you whatever you want to know. Spoken plainly."

"All right. I'll hold you to that. But I warn you, I have lots of questions."

She was thoughtful that afternoon as they worked, and Josh wished he could ask his questions then. He was afraid that in the interim she would have too much time to manufacture answers, none that would do him any good.

There was a crowd at the table at supper, and the talk among the young men and women was how they had spent their last rest day and how they would spend the next.

"What did you do on your rest days where you came from?" Gil asked Josh.

"Studied, mostly. Unless Coach called extra practice. He was always calling for more practice."

"Practicing what?" asked Imelda, her eyes merry.

"Basketball. I also went out for track."

"Track?" asked Gil.

"Running."

Chad Tolliver seemed to be trying to understand. "What is this 'basketball'?"

Kaspar grunted and turned away, as though impatient with their ignorance, but Josh wanted to explain. "It's a game. Most of the high schools have teams. The object is to run down the court with the ball and toss it into the other team's basket. The baskets are made of net, open at the bottom so the ball can fall out again."

"Each team has a ball, and they run around the court trying to throw it in the other's basket?" asked a tall fellow.

"No, there's only one ball. Each team tries to take it away from the other, and there are all sorts of rules about how you can bounce it, run with it, steal it, throw it . . ."

It had begun to sound ridiculous, but Josh continued: "There are points if you score, points if you foul—break a rule—and different points for the type of shot you make—long shot, free throw . . ."

"Then what?" asked Gil.

"What do you mean?"

"After it's over and a team has won, what do you do with the basket?"

"We don't do anything with it. The team that gets the most points wins."

"Wins what?"

"The game!" Josh said in exasperation.

There were chuckles around the table. Imelda began to giggle, she and Sylvania together.

"But what *good* is it?" asked one of the young men. "What does it matter whether you can throw a ball in a basket or not?"

"It's a matter of skill and timing and endurance," Josh explained. "Like the day you were throwing that wood block around. You get better with practice."

Chad leaned forward, his large arms on the table. "I wouldn't like it. I'd rather carry something in my hands I had made—a bench or bed or a wheel or harness. Why go to so much work over a basket with a hole in the bottom?"

At that, the whole table broke into laughter, Mavis, too, and Josh wished he had never brought the subject up.

Kaspar seemed to watch them all from a world within himself. His eyes darted from one to another, and he methodically cracked the knuckles of one hand, then the other, lips barely moving to some internal dialogue. He seemed, for the time being, to have forgotten Josh, and Josh preferred it that way.

After dinner, Mavis went off to bathe at the pump with the other girls, and Josh stuck close to Gil at the river. The young boy was on the chubby side, and though he did not sink when he swam, he fought the water and came up each time gasping for air, worn out with his own exertions.

Josh waded in. "Gil," he said, "you can be a much better swimmer than that. You could be a great swimmer, in fact, but you've got to kick from the hips. That's where your power comes from. And move your legs only far enough to feel your knees pass each other, okay? Come on, try it, and then I'll show you something about your arm stroke."

"You were on a swimming team, too?" Gil asked.

"Yeah, once."

The boy seemed delighted to have Josh as his instructor, and others, Gil's friends, stood in the shallow water watching, imitating the arm movements that Josh was demonstrating.

"Hey, now, that was better! Much better! Try it again," Josh called out to Gil. "Separate your fingers slightly and keep your hands relaxed. Don't hit at the water open-handed like that. You don't have to beat it to death."

The friends laughed, and so did Gil; then he tried again.

As he stood there in the water giving the lesson, Josh realized suddenly that he had not yet tried the river as a way out of Canara. The current was swift but not, to his eye, dangerously so. Nonetheless, not knowing what was downstream, he decided that should he attempt to swim it, he would go straight across to the opposite shore. The length of a football field, perhaps. Piece of cake. He would have to plan this carefully—what to take, what to wear . . .

Leaving the boys to practice on their own, Josh edged back up the bank. When he had dressed, he slipped off by himself to explore some more in the fading light. He particularly wanted to follow the path he had seen leading out of the clearing, a path he was sure was not wide enough for a wagon.

He searched where he thought it had been and, as the light grew fainter still, was beginning to think he was losing his mind, that there was now no path at all; then he finally made it out and, moving swiftly lest anyone see him, parted the bushes and edged his body along the narrow trail.

The trees did not extend as far as he had thought, for after a short distance, instead of the darkness growing blacker around him, he began to see glimpses of sky ahead, as though night were over and dawn beginning again. It was only the contrast, however, for as soon as he came out of the trees, the sky was definitely evening, same as it had been. The landscape before him looked like a battlefield of some past apocalypse. Vines had begun to grow, of course, and small saplings shot up here and there, but when he looked closely, he could see that a fire had once burned the field to the ground, and when he stumbled over something in his path and reached down to pick it up, he discovered a charred door latch and handle. There were more charred beams farther on. A burnt chair, entwined with ivy. A blackened bed frame.

Slowly Josh made his way across the field and discovered a whole village burnt to the ground. A shutter here, a step there, a fence, a gate, a door, a lamp—blackened, rusty, slowly being swallowed up by the meadow.

Something had happened that no one had told him about, and Josh decided it would be the first question on his list when he talked with Mavis.

He looked for her, but she was by the well with the short girl named Helena, laughing and sharing secrets. So, tired anyway, he went back to the stable, took off his sneakers, and stretched out on the burlap-covered straw. It was discouraging how long it was taking his rib to heal. He felt exhausted after only mild exertion.

He had thought he would not fall asleep for an hour or two, but was more tired than he realized. In a few minutes he felt the heavy sensation in his arms and legs that signaled sleep, the numbness of his eyelids, fingers, tongue . . .

Someone had him by the shoulder and was shaking him roughly. In his dream, Josh rolled away from Old Sly's grasp, but the shaking continued still and he opened his eyes to find a boot next to his face. Turning his head, he saw Kaspar. *Oh, no. Not again.*

"Let's talk," Kaspar said, giving him another shake.

Josh grunted and felt his eyes closing again, but Kaspar shook him a third time.

"Are you with me or not?" Kaspar asked.

"I was *asleep*!" Josh said, trying to get his thoughts together.

"You're awake now," Kaspar said, and sat down on an overturned bucket.

"So what do you want from me, anyway? You don't exactly strike me as friendly."

"I'm not interested in friends, I'm interested in getting out," Kaspar said. He swore. "If I was home, I'd be graduating next June."

Josh propped his arms behind his head and struggled to keep his eyes open. "Yeah? What was your major?" he asked sleepily.

"I was going to enter law school. Dad was a criminal lawyer—the best there was. You know the guy in New Jersey who murdered those three women? Guilty as sin? Everybody was talking about the electric chair?"

"When was this?"

"Eight or nine years ago. Well, Dad got him off."

"You bragging or apologizing?"

"That was his job! Somebody had to defend the guy! Dad got him confined to a mental hospital, and now he's in a halfway house."

"And if he murders again?"

"That's not Dad's problem. He did his job, and there're big, big bucks in criminal law."

"Is your father still alive?"

"No. If he was, I'll bet *he'd* find me."

"Well, I don't see how I can help you."

"I figure it all rests on the China boys. When you come right down to it, I'll bet this place isn't different from any other. Everything runs on money. Somebody, somewhere, is on the take, and when we figure out who it is, we offer a bribe."

"You're a great guy, you know it? What makes you think I want to help?"

"Because if you don't, I slit your throat," Kaspar said, and Josh heard the snap of a switchblade.

"You're as crazy as the rest. What good would that do?"

"Be one less person to get in my way. You're

either with me or against me. If you're with me, we can probably get out together. You're against me, you're six feet under and no one will miss you. Think about it."

He was face-to-face with a madman. "So what do you want me to do?" Josh asked, curious despite himself.

Kaspar leaned closer. "I figure Leone's the key. They say she can't talk. Well, she'd talk if she had to. I think she's got a real sweet deal going with the Chinamen. She drags people in here, slave labor, and gets a cut of all the 'sang we dig."

"For what? What does she do with the money? In fact, what do the rest of you do with yours? What can you buy here?"

"We give our orders to Pardo and he gives them to the traders. Except some things we never get. I put in for a transistor radio and never got one. Pardo says it wouldn't work here in Canara, but I don't believe him. Anyway, I'm saving every cent I earn now, and more that I haven't. I ever meet the traders, I'll give it all to them to follow them out. I'll bet that's how the others did it. I may have to bribe Leone first, but I'll do whatever's necessary."

"Then why do you need me?"

"Because you want to get out as badly as I do; if we team up we can get out all the faster. I steal. Everything I can find. I take ginseng from some of the other pouches, too, and get paid for it; all's fair in war, you know. You add your take to mine and the China boys can have it if they'll just lead us out."

"It's not my style," Josh told him.

"It will be," Kaspar said, and his voice was threatening.

"I'll think about it," Josh said. "I'm tired. I want to sleep."

Kaspar leaned closer still. "Tell me now. I've got to plan this carefully . . ."

"Nothing to tell," Josh said, his heart pounding. He could not believe Kaspar could not hear it, the beat was so loud.

A clunking noise at the opposite end of the stable meant that someone was bringing in the last horse for the night. And in that moment, Kaspar was gone. Josh rolled over, waiting for his pulse to subside, but he knew he would not sleep. He'd been convinced that his best hope of leaving Canara was Mavis, that if anyone was to help him, it would be her. Anything Kaspar proposed would make her hate him, and Josh had no intention of letting that happen. At the same time, he wanted to live, and Kaspar meant business.

He sat up, cold sweat on his forehead, a hollow feeling at the back of his throat. *Now.* Swim the river *now.* Without hesitation he got up and put his things, shoes included, in his pack.

Then he walked barefoot out of the stable and down to the river.

Everyone was in for the night, it seemed. The riverbank was deserted. There was no smoke coming from the cookhouse, no banging of pots and pans. The waning moon was now only three-quarters full, sliding in and out of the clouds, and Josh stood on the bank, studying the dark outline of trees on the opposite shore, steeling himself for the swim.

The biggest problem would be to keep his pack from sinking. It was supposedly waterproof, but it wasn't intended to float. He slipped off his jeans, then his shirt, leaving his T-shirt on for warmth, and stuffed the clothes in his pack. Then, with a quick glance over his shoulder, he waded silently into the water until it reached his chest, sucking in his breath with the cold wash of it. Finally, when he could no longer touch bottom, he pushed the pack on ahead of him and began to swim.

The pain! Something about the stretching and breathing brought back the sharp stab in his rib. He quickly gave up the long strokes he had counted on to get himself across and settled for dog-paddling instead. It would take twice as long to get there this way, but it would be easier going. Easier to keep an eye on his pack, too, keep it afloat.

He tried to remember how many strokes it

took to go twenty-five meters on the swim team. Fifteen, perhaps? Twenty? But he had not been dog-paddling or trying to push a backpack ahead of him. It might take him twice as many strokes. If it would have taken a hundred to swim the river without a pack or a broken rib, why not figure that two hundred now would get him to the other side? Three or four hundred, even.

Take your time, he told himself. *Just keep a steady pace, hold the pack up. Don't let it sink. Sixteen, seventeen, eighteen, nineteen . . .*

He was glad he wore the T-shirt, for already he felt chilled. He did not know this river—didn't even know its name—so there might be rocks he had not anticipated, drifting logs, rushes . . . From the bank where he washed in the evenings, he'd seemed to see an expanse of water unbroken by anything that might be a danger. Should be easy going. Still . . .

Thirty-one, thirty-two, thirty-three, thirty-four . . .

Josh could not understand why he was beginning to tire, except that his rib hurt. The cold water didn't help—his body fought it, refused to flow with it. Having to keep a pack afloat was another obstacle he wasn't used to while swimming, basically using only one arm to paddle. He was not in shape, he thought, and mourned the fact that every day spent in Canara, he was losing muscle tone, stamina; he might never make the track and basketball teams once he got to Dallas.

Forty-four, forty-five, forty-six . . .

The pack was beginning to absorb water, and it was harder and harder to keep up. He did the dead man's float from time to time to give his body a rest, but that even made him colder. Every so often he rose up high to see over the top of his pack, to determine when he was halfway there. But in the darkness, this close to the water's surface, he could not tell whether the shadows ahead were trees on the opposite bank or just gloom settling down over the river.

Fifty-nine, sixty, sixty-one . . .

He flopped over on his back and rested the pack on his abdomen. His arms began to flail rather than stroke. He felt they had come unhinged and were slapping at the water without much direction or purpose.

Seventy. Or was it sixty? Had he even done the fifties yet? He was beginning to lose count.

The first sign of panic set in when his teeth began to chatter uncontrollably. What would he do when he got to the opposite bank if there was no road, no cottage, no place to dry himself off and spend the night?

Survival, he told himself. *Quit playing around, now. Swim!*

He cut the water hard, cleanly, renewing his efforts at the backstroke. He tried to hear the admonitions of his old swim coach in his head, telling him what a lousy job he was doing, how to improve.

Ninety-one, ninety-two . . . How could he be up to the nineties already? No, how could he *not* be? Flopping over again, he pushed his pack aside for a clearer view of the opposite bank. Shadows, shadows, but he could make out nothing definite.

His teeth continued to chatter, and his throat felt raw and thick, as though his chest were filling with fluid. He was cold, very cold. How could he have been swimming this long and still not have reached the other side?

There was a sound that suddenly brought his mind into sharp focus. Something up ahead, perhaps? Had someone seen him? A click. A clunk. His body went on full alert.

It came again, and this time Josh realized it was coming from behind. Fear consumed him. Old Sly rowing after him in a fishing boat? Kaspar, swimming with strong muscular arms, knife between his teeth?

He swam harder, faster, but when he heard the noise again, he glanced swiftly over his shoulder.

And then he stopped swimming altogether and slowly turned around. He had not gone more than sixty feet from shore, and there was Pardo, drawing water from the well.

ten

JOSH lay on the straw that night, convinced he would lose his mind. He had lost his moorings, his balance, his compass. There was nothing to hold on to, nothing fixed or sure. He well understood Kaspar's desperation. How could they *not* go mad?

His wet clothes were strewn about the straw, their damp smell filling his nostrils, but Josh was more conscious of the rising panic in his chest. A prisoner, condemned to spend the rest of his life in Canara. BOSTON YOUTH DISAPPEARS ON WAY TO TEXAS. He had never felt so trapped.

Again he thought of Mavis. She had said she would answer anything, though he knew that her answers might not comfort him, much less help. He was as close as he had ever been to despair.

He had intended to be at the wagon early so

he could sit by her on the way to the diggings and ask her to eat with him at noon. But when he woke the next morning, his throat was raw, his head pounded, and he alternately broke into a sweat and shivered with a chill.

Eulaylia laid her hand on his forehead when he entered the cookhouse.

"Joshua, you are burning with fever," she said. "You will not go digging today."

"I'll work it off; it'll be okay," Josh told her. But his words sounded slow, even to himself, and before he had finished his porridge he had to leave the table, and threw up what he had eaten. He went to the well for a drink, then made his way dizzily back to the stable.

He knew that his long exposure in the frigid water the night before was the cause of his shivering, not his stomach. If his stomach churned, it was from anger and disappointment, not the cold.

Still, he huddled down in the straw, sweatshirt over his shoulders, listening to the creak of the wagon wheels as first one wagon, then the next, rolled out of the stable and toward the woods with the 'sang diggers, the plodding sound of the horses' hooves, the occasional snort, and finally, from far off, the singsong chant of young children as they recited their sums from the cookhouse.

He drifted in and out of sleep, perspiring as

the sun came in through the window of the loft and fell full on his face. After a while he felt a terrible thirst that drove him from his makeshift bed and out to the rain barrel for water. Once again the day was unusually warm and muggy— a welcome respite from the cold he had felt when he first arrived. The air was heavy, and clung to skin and clothes.

Josh had just cupped his hands and taken a drink when he heard a soft cry, like a kitten's mew. He drank again, listening, and when the cry came a second time, he wiped his hands on his trousers and followed it into the trees.

His feet took him down a narrow path behind the stable to a tiny cottage almost obscured by thick undergrowth. He felt dizzy, and debated going back to lie down. Still . . .

Josh drew closer and saw no activity near the cottage, heard no other noise. He listened at the door, then knocked lightly, and this time the shutter of a window opened. "Help me!" came a high, tremulous voice, like that of an old woman.

Josh moved toward the window. "What can I do?"

"My water . . . I've spilt it," came the voice, and a thin, clawlike hand appeared on the sill. Beyond the sill, Josh could just make out the top of an ancient head, a few white wisps of hair partially covering a pink scalp. *Isobel, the Old One?*

A second hand appeared and, aided by the first, hoisted an earthenware pitcher to the ledge. Josh took it. "Could you get me more?" she asked.

"Of course," he said. "Would you be Isobel?"

"That is my name."

"I'll be right back," Josh told her. He went immediately to the well and, his body weaving, perspiring, returned with the pitcher. When he passed it through the window, the gnarled old hands clutched at it, pulling it inside, and Josh could hear the noisy sound of the old woman drinking. Her clothes had a stale, unwashed odor.

"Do you need anything else?" he inquired.

"No," she said.

"Would you like me to open some windows for you, then? I'd think you might need some air."

"This old body needs all the warmth it can get," the quivery voice said. "Leone will be here shortly, and she will push me around in the cart to take the air." The head and hands disappeared, slipping slowly out of sight, like someone sinking gently into sleep. But Josh was startled to hear her say, "You are Joshua."

He wished he could see her eyes. "Yes . . . how did you know?"

"Leone found you; I have heard."

"I'm curious why you call me Joshua. I rarely use that name myself."

"But that *is* your name, surely? 'Whom God has saved'?"

The irony of it made him laugh. "It doesn't seem so," he said. And when she made no reply, he asked quickly, "Isobel, may I ask you a question?"

"I am very tired, Joshua. Now that I've had my drink, I would sleep." Her voice was beginning to fade.

"I'll go," he promised, "but please, just one?"

"If I can answer before I sleep . . ."

"Do you know—is there *anyone* here who knows what I must do to leave Canara? I *have* to go. Someone's expecting me."

This time the old woman's voice sounded so drowsy, the words so spaced, that Josh was afraid she would forget the question. "Joshua Vardy," she said, one crooked finger inching itself onto the sill again, as if it had eyes in itself to observe him: ". . . to go forward, you must go back, for you have lost your way." Then the finger relaxed and slipped off the sill, and the smell of her fetid breath lingered above the empty space.

Josh waited at the window a few minutes longer to see if she would speak again, but there soon came a ragged snore from beyond the sill, and finally he went back to the stable and curled up again on the straw.

What did it mean, and how did she know? She had never seen him before. Or did she give out proverbs to whoever came by, like fortunes in a Chinese cookie?

Perhaps Kaspar was right—she and Leone were keepers of the realm. Maybe Leone brought them in and Isobel let them go, and together they cast a spell over Canara, a spell born of 'sang, of rock and river, sun and sky, of mountain trees and winter apples. A witch spell.

Or was it something more—a spirit, a will among all the residents of Canara that held them together, that kept them here, separate from the world? He didn't know, nor was he sure he would ever know.

Isobel's answer certainly made no sense. He was lost, surely, but through no fault of his. Only that he had left the interstate and taken his chances up there in the pass. To go forward he had to go back? To where? She was crazy.

He dozed off once again, then woke briefly when Leone came with a jar of ginseng tea, which she wordlessly held to his lips. It was all he could do to get it down—vile stuff. Then she was gone. Maybe there was something in the tea that kept them docile, confused. Or was it the opposite? Something in the tea that made them stronger? Kept them together? He felt as though he had fallen into a bubble inside earth's atmosphere that had its own rules, its own laws, its own natural properties, with little resemblance to the world he had known back in Massachusetts.

By the time Leone came for the wagon again to take lunch to the diggers, Josh had fallen into a heavy sleep; he slept away the better part of the afternoon, undisturbed by the shouts of children rolling logs down the hill toward the river in play, or the creak of the wagons as they brought the diggers back around five. He slept right through the supper hour, his clothes soaked with sweat, and did not waken again until he felt cool fingers on his forehead and heard Mavis say, "Your shirt is soaked. That means the fever's broken, Josh."

He struggled to open his eyes, then let them close again. Mavis had changed out of her digging clothes and appeared freshly washed and combed.

"I've brought you a leg of chicken and some white beans," she said. "How's your throat? Can you swallow?"

He tried. The pain was not nearly as bad as it had been.

"It's better," he said.

She held out a cup of water. Josh rolled over and sat up, then drank. He did feel better.

"Will you eat?" she asked.

"If you'll stay and talk with me."

"I'll stay," she said, laughing. "I have to bribe you to eat?"

He decided to ease her into the answers he needed, and said, "Tell me the rest of the story about the Melungeons." Settling back against the hay, Josh took a bite of chicken, pulling the meat off with his teeth.

"It will bore you."

"No it won't. Go ahead."

"Well, we first came—our ancestors—from the mountains of Portugal, recruited by Captain Juan Pardo."

"Pardo?"

"Our Pardo is a descendant, he tells us. And we settled the first European colony here— Santa Elena, in South Carolina."

"When was all this?"

"In your year of 1566. When the settlement was overrun by the English, our people escaped into the backwoods, making their way to the mountains of Appalachia. Some married the natives—the Indians."

"And that's who the people of Canara are descended from? The original settlers of Santa Elena?"

"Oh, it's much more complicated than that. Have some beans, Josh. Some milk, too. And there's bread." She reached into the deep pocket of her skirt and produced a sizable chunk. Josh was amazed he had any appetite at all, but it helped to have Mavis to talk with. He concentrated on eating slowly to keep her there.

"Complicated how?" he asked.

"That same year, the English pirate, Sir Francis Drake—and he *was* a pirate, Josh, no matter what else he did—made a raid against the Spanish and Portuguese on the coast of Brazil. He liberated hundreds of prisoners—Moorish and Turkish galley slaves captured in sea battles. There were also South American Indians and West African Muslims . . ." She grinned broadly. "Eulaylia praises me in our history lessons because my memory is good."

"So I see," said Josh, returning her smile.

"Drake planned to release the Turks and Africans on Cuba to defend against the Spanish, but it was stormy, and the ships were blown off course. They were forced up the coast to Roanoke Island. Drake left most of his passengers there, as he was sailing to England, saying he would be back for them. But two weeks later, when Sir Walter Raleigh visited the island, guess what? The people Drake left had vanished."

"What happened to them?"

"Ah!" Josh could tell she liked this part. He wanted to keep her going just to see her eyes sparkle. "They made their way to the mainland, and eventually met up with the survivors of

Santa Elena. We are Christian, Jew, and Muslim, thousands of miles from our home. We are Portuguese, Spanish, Berber, Arab, Jew, and black, yet we all live together peaceably. Well, most of us—Kaspar and a few others excepted."

"But how do you know this is true? I never heard it in school."

"Eulaylia said they don't teach it in schools beyond The Edge. They tell of a place called Jamestown, but the books never mention Santa Elena."

"So when did you start calling yourselves Melungeons?"

"It's the name others called us, and it's not a good one, Josh. To many, a Melungeon is a nobody. Worthless. It's a Turkish word, meaning 'one whose life or soul has been cursed.'"

Suddenly Josh was no longer hungry. The food he had eaten so far seemed to have formed a hardened ball in the pit of his stomach, making it ache. The meaning of his own name, as told to him by Isobel, seemed a joke.

"Is that what we are here—cursed? Is that what I've got to look forward to, Mavis?"

"You could have a lot to look forward to in Canara! Why do you always see only the dark of things? You think it's your ending up here that is the problem, but I tell you it's not. It's what you make of it that's important."

"Then why won't anyone tell me the truth?

How did Leone find me, and why can't I leave?"

"I never said you couldn't. People come to Canara by different ways, and some of the new ones leave again, but none of us know how. We *don't*, Josh! I haven't lied to you. It's just— Eulaylia made us promise that with the new people, we should not tell so much at once. Just a little at a time, until they feel settled."

"How often do you get new people?"

"Not often. Everything has to be just right for it to happen, and only those with Melungeon blood can find their way in."

"I'll never feel settled here!" Josh said angrily. "I'll never feel that this is home."

Mavis looked truly alarmed, and started to get up. "Then I'm sorry I've told you anything at all, and I will never tell you anything again."

Josh grabbed her wrist. "No. Don't go, Mavis. I'm sorry. I'm *trying* to get along. I just want some answers."

"I shouldn't have told you anything," she repeated. "They *said* it might upset you, and after what happened to my father . . ."

Josh gently urged her down beside him again and managed to keep his voice soft and calm. "I won't get upset again. What happened to your father?"

She studied him uncertainly.

"I really want to know," Josh said. "I'll be a lot more upset if you *don't* tell me."

"He went mad, Josh. That's what they say. He loved my mother—he must have—and they thought he was settling in, but he couldn't take not ever leaving Canara; he couldn't find his way out, and one day"—Mavis swallowed—"he got the idea that if he could start a large fire, the smoke might alert the authorities, and someone would come. A rescue plane, perhaps. Forest . . . uh . . . workers? Is that what they're called?"

"Rangers."

"Yes. Rangers. And so, he set a fire . . ." She fell silent, hands in her lap.

Josh guessed the rest. "And it burned the village down?"

"Yes! How did you know?"

"I was out walking and saw the ruins. The charred wood . . ."

"Canara burned to the ground, some of the villagers with it. All had to be rebuilt."

"And your father?"

At this, Mavis got to her feet, stepping on the hem of her skirt in her haste to get away. Josh reached out to hold her back, but she wrestled from his grasp and ran from the stable.

He sat staring after her, then got up and went down to the river, where the men and boys were bathing. He sought out Gil, who was horsing around with the younger boys, and after the soaping was over and bodies were rinsed and glistening, Josh sat on the log beside him as the boy pulled on his boots.

"How much do you know about Canara?" he asked. "Are you any good at history?"

"Not the old stuff," Gil said. "But some things I remember."

"Do you remember hearing about the fire, when Canara burned to the ground?"

"Oh, yes. Eulaylia told me. Just that Jack did it, trying to get someone to come."

"People died in the fire, I heard."

"Yes. Four, I think. Mostly the old, and a child."

"What happened to Mavis's father?"

"He died, too."

"Burned to death?"

"Uh-uh." Gil pulled on his other boot and stopped to tie the lace. "They stoned him. That's how he died."

eleven

HE felt more sympathetic toward Kaspar now. The panic inside Josh's chest had begun to harden into rage. Life presented him with two choices, it seemed—give up and settle in, or live the rest of his life in anger. He had not asked for this—had done nothing to deserve it—and therefore saw no reason to behave any more honorably than he had been treated. Kaspar's point exactly.

Was he dealing with magic here? Illusion? Had he fallen in with some primitive cult? When had the last person in civilized society been stoned to death?

Josh went with the diggers the following day feeling both numb and wary as a rabbit, ready to run. Kaspar seemed to notice, and gave him a cynical smile. He moved up beside Josh when the diggers left the wagon and murmured, "I'm perfecting a plan . . ."

"Sure," Josh said bitterly. "Bribe Leone . . . pay the traders . . . steal the ginseng . . . What else have you tried? Nothing works."

"This will. It's foolproof this time."

"Yeah? What?" Josh glanced at him, and for just a moment felt he was looking into the eyes of the insane. Of course. It had happened to Mavis's father, hadn't it? Now it was happening to Kaspar, and then whose turn would it be?

Kaspar smiled as if to himself. "You'd like to know, wouldn't you? Well, not until I'm ready . . ."

"Fine," said Josh. "Good luck." And they went their separate paths.

At lunchtime, Mavis studied Josh curiously as she ate her bread and grapes. As they returned to the wagon for their pouches and took long drinks from the water barrel, she said, "I'm afraid I upset you yesterday."

"I think *I* upset *you*," Josh replied.

"Talking about my father always upsets me. I didn't even know him, and yet I keep imagining what it must have been like for him."

"I know. Gil told me."

"Oh," she said. Then, "Everything?"

"About the stoning, yes. And that's when your mother stopped talking?"

"That's what they told me. I've never heard her voice. Eulaylia is more my mother than she."

"You sound bitter."

"I do? What's the good of it? But I lost a father, then a mother . . . The way some people talk, he was trying to kill us all. I have even heard it said that he came here to destroy Canara. That wasn't it at all. He didn't *mean* to set the whole village on fire, you know. He just wanted to get back to Beyond. Is that such a terrible thing?"

"You tell me. Have *you* never felt that way?"

"I'd just like to know about other places. Miss Curiosity, Eulaylia called me once. She says we'll be happier if we accept who and where we are, but she has curiosities herself; she told me."

"Yet Leone and Isobel and Pardo meet the traders in a place you call The Edge. Couldn't *they* leave if they wanted?" Josh asked.

"I wish I knew."

A massive body suddenly pushed them apart, and Josh felt himself propelled away from the wagon. He staggered, stumbling until he was able to stop himself by grabbing on to a tree.

Old Sly faced him, nostrils flared, like Goliath prepared to do battle.

"Do you talk or do you work?" the man said huskily.

"I was just getting my pouch to begin," Josh answered.

"A poor job you have done, too." Old Sly's

look was so ferocious that Josh didn't even try to reason with him. Instead he picked up his pouch and found himself moving off in Kaspar's direction.

"You sure rattled his cage," Kaspar murmured.

"He seems to have hated me ever since I came. I don't know why."

"Because you're hanging around his granddaughter, that's why. Or vice versa."

"What's he afraid of?"

"That she'll want to leave. They've got a good thing going here in Canara. Someday we're going to wake up and find that Old Sly and Leone, Pardo and the old crone have absconded with all the money. They'll make some deal with the China boys, and they're out of here. Then we'll be cut off from everything."

"So what's your plan?" Josh asked.

"Break the spell."

"You can't be serious. What do you think it is, witchcraft?"

"Call it what you like. It's not anything they teach at Penn State, I'll tell you that."

"And how will you break the spell?"

"That's for me to know," Kaspar said, and walked away.

Josh returned to his work. The labor was tedious, not in the digging but in the looking. Hours were spent parting the underbrush, searching around tree roots. Only occasionally was a digger rewarded. Rarely did anyone make more than two finds in one day.

He sat silently in the wagon going back that afternoon, conscious of Old Sly's eye on him. Let the man suspect what he would; Josh would not try to take Mavis, and he didn't relish the idea of escaping with Kaspar, either. When he left, he would go alone—silently, unexpectedly, with no good-byes. He had his own plan—to go back to The Stop and look for railroad tracks or the remains of a road, then follow them until they took him somewhere.

Mavis began singing softly as soon as the village came into view. Josh had noticed this before. She seemed to do it spontaneously, as though suddenly filled with a great joy. He wished he could feel even a fraction of her happiness.

He sat with Gil at supper, listening to the young lad chatter away about a game he had invented using stones and sticks and acorns. Afterward the younger boys whooped and tussled in the water, sending as much soap floating downriver as they got on their skin. The oldest men, because of the coldness of the water or their shyness about their wrinkled bodies, often waded in up to their knees with their britches still on, their boots and shirts left on the bank, and stood in soggy trousers, soaping their chests and armpits.

Josh left the river early, dressed, and slipped away. He finally found the path that the young people had used to go to The Stop, and set out.

It was still light enough that no lantern was needed. He could see where the weeds had been trampled down by their footsteps, the low-hanging bush where Gil, in a moment of youthful exuberance, had leaped into the air and tried to chin himself. Josh did not saunter along as he had that night, however. This time there were no bobbing lanterns to light his path, and he wanted to get there while he could still see the ground. He realized with dismay that he had set off without his pack.

Go on, he decided. Go without any possessions at all, if there was something to follow. He would rather spend a miserable week or more getting to Texas than risk going back for his plane ticket.

He remembered how excited he had been that night when he mounted the crest of the hill and saw the roadside restaurant below, all lit up—as though he were waking from a bad dream and finding himself back in familiar territory. How hope had drained out of him when he discovered there was no phone. No people. A ghost town.

He quickened his pace as he recognized a landmark—a ragged jutting rock onto which some of the young men had climbed, pounding their chests and leaping down, egged on by the laughter of the girls. He remembered how Sylvania's high-pitched giggle had risen above the rest, the way she had smiled sideways at Josh, encouraging him to make her laugh.

And yes, there was the field of small purple wildflowers, the aging oak, and, just beyond, the peeling sycamore, with leaves like Old Sly's hands, large and brown and dry. Then the fence they'd had to crawl over, the hill they'd had to climb . . .

Josh broke into a trot, then a run, his rib hurting with every jostling step, but he couldn't hold back. Up over the top, and then . . .

He stopped, steadying himself against the rock face. There was no roadside café; no road, no sign.

Uttering a cry, he went slipping and sliding down the short hill and stared at the place he was sure the restaurant had been. Was *positive* it had been. He turned slowly around to check his location, to see if possibly the café had been off to one side or the other. No, it had been here, *here* that they had danced and the dulcimers had thumped, here that the girls had laughed and tossed their hair, and Kaspar had caught him by the throat. All gone without a trace. Not even a bare spot in the grass. Weeds covered the ground as though they had grown here always.

Josh threw back his head and howled at the

sky. His voice, echoing back at him, had such a desperate ring that he brayed again to see if the echo could possibly be his.

This must be the way it happened, then—the way they all went mad. One reality after another would be taken away from him until all he knew was the spell he was under, and then it would cease to be strange.

Catching his breath, he ran off to the right like a bloodhound, searching for old railroad tracks. A rusty switch. A bolt. A pin. Nothing. Then he ran to the left, falling to his knees, finally, tearing at the undergrowth with his hands. Nothing, nothing.

Josh flung himself backward onto the ground and stared up at the buzzards circling overhead in the evening air. A sound he had never heard before came from his throat—a rasping croak, so hopeless and distressed that gooseflesh rose on his arms. The sound came again, as though his body were turning to buzzard and in time, when it was all too late, he would fly off.

Closing his eyes for a few minutes, he lay still, and when he opened them again, Pardo was looking down at him.

Josh didn't get up. He didn't move, just watched as the man with the copper skin edged over to the stump of a tree and slowly lowered himself, twigs snapping as his boots made nesting places in the underbrush.

For a long time, neither of them spoke, and Josh wondered if they ever would. He himself had nothing to say. Words, along with his strength, had run out.

Finally Pardo said, "You wonder why you are here."

Silence. Why comment on the obvious?

"You are here because you are Melungeon, because we are every man who has ever lost his way, every race who has ever lost its compass. That you should have come along at the exact second you did, in the exact place . . . only the merest chance there was it could have happened to you, Joshua; yet we were there at that same moment, and took you in."

"I didn't lose my way," Josh said, forcing the words through reluctant lips. "I knew exactly where I was headed. I was mugged."

"Ah, yes." Pardo grew thoughtful. "We go so far back, Joshua, that everyman's story is our own."

"Cursed, that's what!" Josh was bitter.

"Cursed and blessed both, perhaps."

"How do you figure that?"

"We have been robbed, ridiculed, converted, murdered—*think* of it! And yet . . . we continue to exist. Destroy us in one place, we pop up in another. Lost, perhaps, but indestructible."

"I don't know anything about this historical

stuff," Josh told him. "Nobody was against me where I came from, and I'm not prejudiced against anyone else. All I want is to get out of Canara and get back in school. I don't even know what month it is. If it's September, I've missed a lot already. Just tell me the truth about what I have to do to get out of here. *Can* I get out?"

"Some do," said Pardo. "A few who came here from Beyond. We never know. One day they're here, the next they're not. Old Isobel knows, perhaps; she keeps track of things like that. We who were born in Canara can never leave, it seems. I accept. I just accept. Most of us, you see, have no wish to leave. We are the fortunate ones."

"But *why* couldn't you leave if you wanted to? What keeps you here in Canara? Do you even know?"

"Only a guess. That there were other groups of Melungeons who fared better than we, I've no doubt. Perhaps they are all assimilated by now, and you couldn't even find them if you tried. But our own little band of people was pushed so far, so deep into the mountains that we were lost to time and space. We have continued to exist in our own little orbit, it would seem, with its own rules and physical properties, its own laws. Were we to leave, we would not exist at all."

"What do you mean? What are you—spirits?" And when Pardo didn't answer, Josh answered for him: "Hardly. If you have lived so isolated in your own little world, how did you hook up with Chinese traders? How did you learn about ginseng? How long has this arrangement been going on?"

"For as long as anyone can remember—beyond remembering."

"But how did it all begin? There has to be a beginning to this lost world, if that's what it is."

"Do you know your own beginnings, Joshua? Do you know with certainty your own changeover between oblivion and consciousness, of nonexistence and physical presence? I don't pretend to know all the answers. Canara is carried along like a leaf in a stream, but for you it is different."

"Does Isobel have anything to do with my being here?"

"She would tell you that Canara is a place for healing. A way station. A respite."

"But does she have the secret to my leaving?"

Pardo grew thoughtful again. "She's almost blind, but still, she sees inside you. It's a gift. She's very old, Joshua. Older than the moon, we say."

"I didn't do anything to deserve being a prisoner in this place."

"Did any of us ever deserve the life we got, good or ill? Does a prince *deserve* to be royalty just because he was born to a queen? Does a man deserve to be persecuted because of his skin? We do not keep you here, Josh. You are as free to go as any of us."

"Then why, when I try, can't I leave?"

"I wish I could tell you, but I don't know. If I could point the way out, I would do it freely. Perhaps you are not yet ready."

"What gives you the right to direct my life, to determine when I'm, as you say, 'ready'?" Josh asked angrily. "*All* of you are crazy. You must think Canara's some sort of Utopia or something. That you've got all the answers."

"Far from it. We're evolving, too. It's only recently we gave up stoning, you see. Before that, it was burning. I'd like to think we've learned a little something. We did not *bring* you here, Josh. We did not ask for you, and certainly not for Kaspar. It just happens. You were found at The Edge and were brought to the village, that's all. You came, and we must all make the best of it. If we can help, we will, but you make the final choices."

More silence. Josh realized after a time that his clothes were soaking up the dew and slowly rose to a sitting position.

"How is it that Isobel knows all about me?" he asked.

"Not all. She only sees farther inside us than we do ourselves, for the old have special powers. Sometimes, if she happens to like you, she may be helpful. If not . . . She's never liked Kaspar much."

"Kaspar doesn't especially like her."

"No, I suppose not."

"What about you, Pardo? How long have you been in Canara?"

"Always," the man replied. "As far back as you can count, my people came from Canara."

"So, if no one here will release me, all I can do is wait?" Josh asked, incredulous.

"Sometimes waiting is hardest of all," Pardo said.

Josh got to his feet. "I wish Leone had left me where she found me. I would have made out okay. I wasn't so badly hurt I couldn't have survived. She had no right to bring me here, involve me in all this."

"She had no choice, lad. It was that one-in-a-million second when your paths crossed. What happens now is up to you."

twelve

HE was beginning to feel more like Kaspar every day. Bitter. Angry. Desperate. School had probably started by now in Dallas. Undoubtedly the track and basketball teams had had tryouts. If he stayed in Canara much longer, he'd be too out of practice to compete. From high school athlete of the year in his old school to a nothing.

Josh walked back to the village alone, for Pardo had disappeared into the early darkness. He was remembering the time he had scored seventeen points in the first quarter, had taken a time-out, and when Coach put him back on the floor, the gym rang with the chant, *"Var-dy! Var-dy! Var-dy!"*

He pressed his lips together and shut his eyes momentarily. Who was he kidding? Probably the only reason he'd been a star back home was that he got some lucky breaks on the floor; the other guys fed him shots. Maybe his team had been so hot last season because the others in its division were so lousy. He might get to that big high school in Dallas and be laughed off the floor during tryouts. He was fast, but he wasn't tall; a sure shooter at the free-throw line, but he rarely made the three-pointers.

Face it: He was scared to death about going to Texas. Starting all over again in the best of circumstances would be hard enough, but to lose his mom and his home at the same time . . . he didn't think he could do it. Inside he felt like an open wound that would never, ever heal. He could feel his heart racing, something he'd been experiencing more and more lately, whenever he thought of his future.

Josh wiped his eyes quickly with an angry swipe of his fingers. He could not afford to feel sorry for himself. He recalled Coach's words: *Nobody ever got to the top on "sorry."* The thing of it was, he would give up all hope of ever playing again, all past and future successes, just to have his mother back. That was the bottom line. One thing he could say about Canara—it sure helped take his mind off the accident. A place for healing, Pardo had called it. It would be so easy to stay here forever, so comforting, in a way, to give up.

No! he told himself, furious for even thinking it. He had one more thing to try. Somewhere near Canara there were dogs, and nobody talked about them. Josh could remember the direction from which their sound had come, and he determined that the next chance he got, he'd check it out.

The sky was about dark when he got back to the village. Mute Leone, Isobel's guardian now, was wheeling the old woman about the village on their evening stroll, caring for her as she had once been cared for herself, Josh decided. As far as anyone else could see, Isobel was merely an unmoving heap of rags, but the tenderness with which her guardian reached down and touched her from time to time seemed to prove that Leone had found in the aged woman someone in whom she could trust.

Canara was shutting down for the night. A few villagers drew water from the well or led the horses in from pasture. The milkers were leaving the cow barn, buckets in either hand. As Josh headed for the stable, someone fell in beside him. It was Mavis.

"You're angry with me," she said.

"Not you," he answered dully. "The situation."

"You can either be angry and turn out like Kaspar or you can settle in and make the best of it," she told him.

"Those are my only choices?"

"What else? *I've* settled."

"You were born here."

"That doesn't mean I've never wanted to go Beyond. We learned something about it in history, though Eulaylia never talks of it except in the past. But if we once came from other places—our people, I mean—those places must be there yet. *You* came from another place."

"Yet you never ask me about it."

"I'm afraid."

"Of what?"

"That I'll want to know more. And so I don't ask. Pardo taught us that."

"How can you go your whole life not knowing?" he asked, a trace of exasperation in his voice. "What kind of life is that?"

"See? I shouldn't be talking to you at all. My grandfather was right: I want to be happy, and I won't if I want what I can't have."

Josh just shook his head.

"Besides," Mavis continued, "I'm not sure that I do want anything else. I belong here, I guess. For centuries, Eulaylia said, we belonged nowhere. No one wanted us. No one believed us. They didn't know what we were. Free persons of color, they called us, but we couldn't vote or own land. I don't mind being here, really. I *like* being Melungeon, and Canara is ours."

"I'd think it would be part of your education to know more."

They walked to the cookhouse, where the cooks were putting the last of the pans away for

141

the night, and sat on a bench at one end of the empty hall, leaning back against a table.

"All right. I'll get brave and ask," Mavis said with sudden determination. "What is this place like where you come from? Is everyone happy and kind and peaceful, and no one ever hungry or cold?"

"In that it's not different from here. You read about bad things in every newspaper. I was beaten up, remember, and left by the road."

"Then why do you want to go back?"

"Because it's the world I knew. I belonged there. I had friends."

"See? *This* is the world *I* know, and I have friends. You would make friends here, too. I'm already your friend."

"Here it's as if I'm in a bubble, Mavis. Don't you feel it? You can go only so far and no farther, and then these invisible walls hold you back. This . . . this aura . . . this force . . . this heaviness in the air . . ."

"A world within a world, Pardo says. That's what Canara is. It's what we learned in school. What did *you* study?"

"Mostly science. Biology, chemistry. I'm planning to be a sports doctor. *Was,* anyway. An orthopedist, maybe."

"I'd rather learn about people. Not their bodies, but their minds."

"Then you'd want the humanities. Psychology, the way people think. Sociology, the way they behave in groups. Sometimes people do things in groups they wouldn't do alone."

"Like what they did to my father," Mavis said.

Josh put his arm around her. "Yes, things like that." He felt very kind toward Mavis, grateful that she had helped pull him out of his dark mood, and wondered if this was what it was like to have a sister. *She'd make a great girlfriend for a wrestler,* he was thinking. For a linebacker on the football team. Mavis with her broad shoulders and hands, her sturdy thighs and feet—pretty in a healthy sort of way.

She didn't move away from him—seemed as comfortable with Josh's arm around her shoulder as Josh did placing it there.

"And what is this place like where you're going? Dallas?" she asked.

"I've only been there a couple of times. Aunt Carol's got this big house—it's nice. But I don't think I'll like Texas much."

"Why not?"

He had to think about it a minute. "In Massachusetts I knew who I was. Where I fit in—at school, I mean. The community. Now I'm going to this place where no one knows anything about me, and I doubt that they'll care. I've got to start all over. I probably don't look like anyone there, and my accent will be different.

But I didn't have a choice in the matter. It's all been done *to* me. Something just swept in and changed my life."

Mavis nodded, saying nothing.

"It's losing Mom that's the hardest, though."

"I understand that, too."

"I forgot. Of course you do." He was quiet for a moment, then continued. "As far as school, well, where I lived your junior and senior years are your best. Everything I've worked for so far was supposed to pay off big time in my last two years of high school. A college scholarship, the works. And now that I'm about there—*this!*"

Mavis drew her feet up on the bench beside her and rested her chin on her knees. "I don't know if I would like that—everything coming down to two . . . what do you call them . . . years? I think I would like my life spaced out—as it is here. I'd like to live it more evenly, I think."

"But if you stay here, what will happen to you?"

"Like all the other girls, I will marry."

"Children?"

"Perhaps, perhaps not. New babies are frowned upon, because livable land is scarce. We try to keep the population stable, producing only enough children to replace the old who die. But I will be around children anyway, for Eulaylia is training me to teach history to the younger ones. When the autumn equinox comes, we'll have more books."

"Why's that?"

"When the ginseng harvest is over, our true classes begin. And on the autumn equinox, for that one day, we will all go to the schoolhouse."

"Like The Stop? It's here for one day and then it disappears? How can that be?"

"Pardo explained it once, but I'm not much good at science. It's like anything else . . . What happens to a full moon? What happens to a storm? A sunset? Where do they go?" She shrugged. "They all come back again in their own time. Canara is in its own little orbit in the place where the Melungeons settled, but it moves around. We are always somewhere in Appalachia, but just where we are at a given time I don't know for certain. Does it matter?"

It matters, thought Josh. And then, with a sudden, growing excitement he dared not let show, *It matters!* His mind raced on ahead of him. If one day the schoolhouse was in Canara and the next day it was not, it must be back outside again, in the place Mavis called Beyond. And everything in it must go back outside, too. If he, for example, were to remain in the schoolhouse after the others left, this might be his ticket to civilization.

Another thought: perhaps it didn't disappear. Perhaps it was there all the time, and this is what the dogs were guarding. Maybe the schoolhouse was the gateway to the world beyond, where Leone met the traders. Once again, he began to hope.

But his explorations were put on hold, for on the next rest day Sylvania and Tom were married. It was announced at breakfast, and as far as Josh could see, there were no elaborate preparations being made. The women made their lye soap as usual, and the village tended to everyday chores.

About noon, however, the pace picked up. Two of the pigs were slaughtered and their carcasses then roasted slowly over an open pit. The aroma seemed to bring life to the village. Children gathered around to watch the basting, and the older girls went to the cabin where Sylvania lived, bringing with them ribbon and squares of handmade lace.

Once again, the day was warm, but with the kind of sky that told of change. They all seemed to know that this would be the last warm night for a long while, and made every excuse to stay outdoors. While Sylvania was being bedecked in lace, Tom—a slim, handsome young man—was engaged in a wrestling match with his old friends down by the river. Stripped to their waists, the men rolled and jostled and laughed, as though Tom were signaling to every rival he'd ever had that Sylvania was now his, and her lips belonged to him alone. Then they washed, dressed, and gathered in the clearing. Sylvania came dressed in bright colors, specially dyed cloth that had been subject to no washings yet. Her red and yellow dress, lace, and scarves completely covered her body, and her hair was festooned with ribbons.

Josh recognized everything and nothing in the ceremony. There was a canopy under which the bride and groom were to stand, symbolic, he thought, of a Jewish ceremony; a cross held by Pardo was such as might appear in a Christian wedding; drums provided the music afterward for the dancing, in which mostly the men took part, reminiscent of a Mideastern custom; and the roasted pigs for the feast, Josh decided, was the usual banquet food of none of the above. Though Pardo officiated during the nuptials, the public declaration by the couple that each was the other's intended seemed sufficient, and here in Canara, at least, Tom and Sylvania were officially wed.

When the women joined the dancing, Sylvania danced with every man in turn, Tom with all the women, and finally, when they went off to the woods for their wedding night in a small cabin a family had lent them, the whole village followed after and stood around the outside singing and calling, some rattling the door handle as if to go in, until finally Tom came to the door and offered sweets to all. Thus satisfied, the crowd dispersed.

Mavis, smiling, clutched Josh's arm as they left the woods and purposefully guided him toward the river.

"Where are we going now?" he asked.

"To swim," she said.

"What? Now?"

"Just come," she whispered, laughing.

The older people and children had gone in for the night, and Eulaylia and Daniel were carving the remaining meat off the pigs. They smiled at the silent parade of single folk who were slipping down to the river's edge. There, Josh was startled to see them quickly disrobe, male and female alike, and slip into the water. He turned to ask Mavis what it was all about, and was astonished to see her pulling her dress over her head, emerging naked in the moonlight, half of her breasts in shadow. Feeling curious, excited, and somewhat awkward, Josh took off his clothes also and ducked into the water behind her.

The coldness of the water took care of any thoughts he might have had of sex. He wasn't sure what he expected would happen next, but in truth, nothing much did. The line of naked figures slowly moved deeper and deeper into the water until most were in up to their waists, some to their shoulders. There were giggles and whispers as the water reached their chins, and the river at last became a shadowy sea of bobbing heads.

Josh had felt embarrassed at first facing Mavis in his nakedness because of the strapping of his chest and the way the cold had shrunk his genitals. But finally, when the river covered them both, he managed to say, through chattering teeth, "What is this? This ceremony?"

"I don't know," she said. "It doesn't have a name. We just always do it—the single people—after a summer wedding, anyway. And some nights just for fun. Eulaylia says more people get engaged in the water after a wedding than at any other time." She laughed. "Daniel says it's a way to see the merchandise before you buy it."

"Then the parents don't mind?"

"They did it themselves. It's tradition."

Josh couldn't help smiling to himself. Parents here were no different from parents anywhere. *Tradition, my foot!* he thought. It was a safe way to cool fevers that might have arisen outside the honeymoon cabin, imagining the pleasures within, that's what. It was the equivalent of a cold shower. He noticed that Imelda had small breasts like lemons, and also, that Chad Tolliver was admiring Mavis whenever she turned.

"Are there ever babies conceived on this night?" he asked her.

She laughed again. "Sometimes. Such things never happen in Boston?"

"Of course. It's the same the world over."

Couples had paired off, talking in low voices, kissing in the water, but the cold soon had them all on the bank, reaching for their clothes, and Josh enjoyed the last fleeting glimpse of feminine arms and legs as dresses were pulled on over heads. What a strange custom—skinny-dipping after summer nuptials! Something else to talk about when he got to Texas.

Mavis had run off with the girls, Chad Tolliver and some of the boys following at a distance—teasing, calling. As Josh put his shoes back on, he saw Gil looking after the group enviously.

The boy came over and stood beside him as Josh stood up and buttoned his shirt.

"I wish there was a special girl for me," he said with a frankness Josh found appealing.

Josh studied him fondly. "There will be. I can almost promise you that."

"Aw, I'm too round, I think," Gil told him.

"You mean fat?"

"Yes. My belly shakes when I walk. I have cheeks like apples." He puffed out his cheeks, then poked at them disgustedly with two fingers. "I dreamed once about lying in bed with a girl. It was even better than I thought."

Josh smiled. "That must have been some dream!"

"I'm too round," Gil said again. "Daniel tells me to hike more and swim, but now that the dark season is coming, the river will be too cold."

"You could always take up track. That would burn off some fat."

"Running? Like you did?"

Josh nodded.

"When will you teach me?"

"I don't know. How about tomorrow morning before the diggers go out? Before breakfast."

"I'll meet you at the cookhouse," Gil said excitedly.

Lying in his bed in the straw that night, Texas on his mind, Josh was pleased that he was thinking *when* again, not *if*. He had not given up. That would be the worst thing he could do. There were still two possibilities to explore—the barking dogs and the schoolhouse. Yet when he woke the next morning, the first thing on his mind was meeting Gil at the cookhouse. He was surprised to discover that he was looking forward to the lesson, that he *wanted* to do this for the boy, and was surprised again, when the session was over, that he had enjoyed it as much as he did, that he took such pleasure in Gil's gratitude. *Some*thing was beginning to heal, he thought.

The next evening after dinner, Josh saw something he had not noticed before. As he rinsed off his plate in the tub by the kitchen door, he saw Old Sly receiving a bucket of meat scraps from the cook. A word, a nod, a handshake, and then Old Sly was out the door, walking swiftly toward a path behind the well. Josh followed.

The big man was walking fast enough that his footsteps made more noise than Josh's, so trailing him was easy. The undergrowth, dense and thick, kept Joshua well-hidden, yet he could follow the soft crunching sound made by Old Sly and, now and then, through the trees, he could see the faded blue of the man's shirt.

It was a path that forked off into a still more obscure path, and then again to a path more hidden yet, seemingly away from the river. But as this one began to angle downward, Josh was excited to see that they were nearing water again, and realized that the river wound around Canara so that there were whole parts of it he had not yet explored. He was sure of it when he saw an old bridge, a long bridge, below.

Made of stone, the surface crumbling, it extended from an outcropping of rock on this side of the water to one on the other. And beyond that rose the opposite shore, its high rocky walls etched against the darkening sky. This side of the bridge was blocked, however, by a tall fence of wire, barbed at the top, and waiting there behind the fence were five of the most ferocious-looking dogs Josh had ever seen. Their bodies were as tense as cocked pistols, heads alert, ears erect, and as soon as Old Sly came into view, they immediately set up a yelping and snarling that was silenced at once by a single word from the man: "Basta!"

Old Sly went up to the fence and threw pieces of meat over the top. The dogs commenced to growl and fight among themselves until all the meat had been devoured. Then they sat down on their haunches to lick their chops.

Expecting Old Sly to turn and head back when the pail was empty, Josh watched as the large man made his way clumsily down the bank instead and rinsed out the bucket in the water. Then he stood for a time staring out across the water toward the other end of the bridge, his body motionless, the air about him still. Even the dogs were silent.

The Edge, Josh thought. This had to be it! Why else the guard dogs, the barbed wire? He waited, moving slightly in the brush to get a better view of Old Sly's face. And then he saw it— the glint of metal reflecting the setting sun. The object lay just beyond Old Sly's feet, and when

Josh moved forward once again, he saw what it was. An oarlock. A boat.

Yes! He would stay here all evening if necessary, until Old Sly went back. There were still several hours of daylight left. The sun was sinking behind the trees, but it would stay light even so.

Old Sly turned finally, and began the climb up the bank, the dogs pacing the bridge overhead. They did not bark this time, but whined and pawed at the fence, wanting to be let out. Old Sly did not oblige them.

Josh lay down in the undergrowth, making himself as flat as possible. He heard Old Sly's steps approaching, and not too far from him the footsteps paused. Josh stopped breathing entirely until he heard the man panting from the exertion of the climb. Finally Old Sly coughed, cleared his throat, and with a small grunt, moved on again. Gradually the footsteps died away.

Not until he was positive that the man had gone did Josh even allow himself to move. Then he got to his feet and started toward the bridge. He had not gone ten yards before the dogs, which had been roaming about behind the barbed wire, heard him and turned, alert. Josh froze.

They had seen him, but they did not bark. Josh and the animals stood facing each other, he at the top of the bank, the dogs on the bridge. They could have been carved from stone, they were so motionless.

Josh eased his body forward one foot. The dogs watched. Waited. The other foot. Silence. Slowly, slowly, one step at a time, Josh inched his way forward. The dogs monitored his progress, small eyes watching through the barbed wire fence.

A step, two steps more, waiting—expecting the ruckus to begin—Josh continued his slow journey, but the dogs remained silent. He made a point of going down the bank some yards away from the bridge so as not to excite them, and then began moving along the edge of the water toward the bridge itself. He could see only the tip of the boat in the rushes, and his heart began to pound.

Above him, the dogs came to the edge of the bridge, their muzzles protruding from openings in the old concrete wall as though sniffing his intent. It wasn't until he walked beneath them, disappearing from their view entirely, that the night air was split apart with a sudden spasm of barking. Each bark drove the others to wilder agitation, their sound rising higher and higher until the noise became a frenzy.

Josh lunged toward the boat. There were two boats, actually, one farther along the bank, and for a moment he considered rowing the one and towing the other so he could not be followed.

There wasn't time. Quickly he unfastened

the closer one and shoved it into the water, then climbed in and pushed. The oars hit bottom as he pulled, but then the boat glided out, the oars cut the water, and finally he was moving away from shore, from the bridge and the dogs, from whomever the barking might have aroused.

He gripped the oars firmly and watched the trees drift farther and farther away.

Good-bye, Canara!

thirteen

HIS biggest fear was not what he would do without his pack and airline ticket, but that he would row for twenty minutes and find he was no closer to the opposite shore. Every time he looked over his shoulder, however, the gray silhouette of trees behind him loomed taller and taller, while the bank he was leaving drifted farther and farther away.

He considered going downriver instead of across. It would soon be night, though, and he couldn't see. If there were rocks, if there were rapids, he was in danger of losing his life. The men, who knew the river, would surely follow. But if he made it across and found anyone at all who could hide him, he would be better off.

Josh frowned as he rowed. Why did he imagine he would be pursued? Hadn't they said he was free to leave? That there were no locks, no walls? Then he remembered the fence with the barbed wire on top, the dogs. Undoubtedly he was nearing The Edge. It was a certainty the men would follow.

The dogs had stopped barking now. At least, he could no longer hear them, and Josh angled the boat slightly downriver, away from the bridge. The current was swifter than he had thought, so that he was rowing against it to make the crossing. He was glad for the exercise, feeling the strain in his delts and pecs, encouraged by the strength of his biceps, glad there was something left of his old self.

Josh rowed with an intensity he had not felt for some time, and was aware, with each stroke, that the air seemed heavier, the atmosphere strangely thick about him.

Finally he felt one oar touch bottom, then the other. The boat tilted slightly as one end ran aground. The land was higher here than it had been on the other side, and Josh had to scramble to climb the bank, trying to see if there was a path he might take.

He knew he had no time to waste, for undoubtedly the men of Canara had heard the barking and would have come to investigate. If ever Josh needed his legs, it was now.

It was soon obvious, however, that he would go nowhere very fast if he tried to go through the woods, for his feet were immediately entangled in vines and undergrowth, and without a lantern, he could not see the many obstacles that lay before him. He remembered the rocky walls he had seen from the other side, and knew he could well end up in a ravine.

All right, he'd take the shoreline. He would follow it until he came to a road, a ramp, a cabin, a fishing camp—anything that would lead him to people. He made his way back down to the water's edge and the narrow strip of land that lined the river.

From far away, Josh heard the barking begin again, and knew that someone had come. He began to run.

Running felt even better than rowing. His muscles, while more sluggish than he had hoped, responded with pleasure, and Josh rejoiced to feel his pulse increasing, his back beginning to perspire, his chest swelling as his lungs inflated, then deflated. Even his rib gave him less trouble than he had imagined.

He still had to be careful where he went, for although it was lighter here than in the woods, there were tree roots and rocks to be reckoned with, and every so often one foot went into the water.

Josh wished that he had not been quite so eager to run once he left the rowboat—that he had at least taken a look at the sky to fix his bearings, remember which way he was headed, should he need to know that again. Had the Big

Dipper been to the left or the right of Venus? Somehow he had placed the planet in a different location than he found it now.

On and on he went, until his lungs begged for relief, and he began to slow, to trot, to walk; at last, bracing one hand against the trunk of a tree, he stopped, chest heaving, to catch his breath.

Following the shoreline might get him nowhere—how likely was he to find a cabin right at the water's edge?—yet it seemed madness to attempt the woods. He would not be able to see the sky, to navigate at all with the stars obscured. He was probably all right now. He'd had a good head start so that even if they were to follow he would soon outrun them.

And then he heard it—the yipping and yelping of dogs. His mouth went dry as his body tensed and turned. How could they be so close to him already when he had run all this way? And why so eager to get him back?

Hide. He scrambled up the bank and into the trees, exploring the darkness with his hands, scouting out each step with one foot before moving his body forward. There were night sounds—croaks and chirps, scurryings and rustlings—but even closer now, the barking of dogs.

He thought of climbing a tree, but rejected the idea just as quickly. He would be trapped like a possum while the pack surrounded the trunk, waiting till the men of Canara arrived to bring him down.

Think. His only hope, as he saw it, lay in diving into the river and hiding until the search was called off. But he had turned only halfway around when he discovered himself in the light of a lantern and, shielding his eyes, found he was looking into the face of Old Sly.

A large hand reached out and roughly seized his clothes, jerking him forward so swiftly that Josh could smell the man's breath in his nostrils.

He could have fought, could have jerked himself free, but the growls of the approaching dogs told him how futile the effort would be. And something more—the fury on Old Sly's face, fury mixed with such sadness that Josh remained immobile till Pardo, holding the dogs on a leash, came crashing through the woods and caught up with them.

It was Pardo who spoke first. "You are ordered to stand trial," he said, tugging at the dogs, which strained to devour Josh. Old Sly still held on to Josh's shirt, and could well have fed him to the animals if he wished.

"For what?" Josh asked. "Trying to save my own life? For trying to find my way out of Canara?"

"For losing a boat, lad. You took a boat and lost it," Pardo said.

"I borrowed it, that's all. I can show you right where I left it."

"We know . . . where you left it," Old Sly said, panting slightly. "We watched you . . . go ashore. But you didn't tie up, and it's drifted downriver."

"It was only a rowboat," Josh protested.

"We had just the two," said Pardo. "We'll have to build another, and ask the traders for oarlocks."

"Then let's go after it. The river doesn't flow *that* fast."

Old Sly released Josh's shirt, but continued to hold the lantern so they could see each other's faces. His voice was strangely gentle.

"A boat without a passenger goes Beyond," he said. "A man from Canara stays in Canara. I have tried it many times."

"You mean if I had rowed downstream, I wouldn't have moved, really? I would still be in Canara?"

"That's true."

"But there must be a point in the water where Canara meets the outside. Where you see fishermen or other boaters. Don't you ever call out to them?"

"That would be The Edge," Pardo explained. "But that is not here."

"Then where are we now?" Josh asked, confused.

"An island, only an island, and Canara still. You have been going in a circle."

Josh refused to believe it. He *wouldn't*. "Then why the dogs and the fence?"

"Look." Old Sly bent down then, lowering the lantern to the ground, and Josh saw that the forest floor was covered with ginseng. He stared at the profusion of plants—thousands and thousands, he guessed. Acres of ginseng. A spell of 'sang. He looked again at Pardo.

"Our bank," Pardo said. "Our future. It's all we have to trade."

"But why, then, do you spend hours looking for it across the river?"

"Because what grows on the other side is almost enough to sustain us. To dig only this— perhaps the largest growth of wild ginseng in the world—would be to spend what should be our children's inheritance. We must protect it, and so we take only the tallest plants from here each digging season, leaving the rest."

"I wasn't after your ginseng. I didn't even know it was here!" Josh protested. "I can't believe that no one else in the village has ever rowed over to see what the dogs were guarding."

"No need," said Pardo. "They know what is here."

"But it's crazy!" Josh exclaimed. "If this belongs to everyone, and no one can leave Canara, why are you so worried about someone taking it? Who would steal from their own safe?"

"So far, no one has, but it's possible that other Melungeons, who don't even know their heritage, might get in somehow and find it. They are the only ones who could. Some time back, a drunken band of Melungeons stumbled into Canara, raised a ruckus for a while, and wandered out again. Whether this was possible because of their physical state, we don't know, but it left us shaken. We never knew what happened to them, but could hear their rowdy singing long after they were out of sight. A few of our young men, of course, tried to follow and found themselves back at the barn." Pardo sighed. "Though no one has raided Canara before, there is always that possibility through means we don't understand, so we take no chances."

And then, noticing that Josh was again studying the dogs, Pardo said, "They bark when someone new, like yourself, goes near the bridge. Or when they hear, from far off, people approaching The Edge. It doesn't happen often, and when it does, it's just outsiders, exploring, lost. They wander into The Edge and out again, never knowing where they were, and we go on as before."

They hiked back to where the second boat, tied to a pillar, waited at the bridge. Old Sly guided Josh onto a seat, holding fast to his arm. The dogs whined when the men got in, and Pardo unleashed them, leaving them behind. As the boat glided away from the bank, the dogs raced back up on the bridge and followed the men across the water, yelping and snarling, toward the fence on the other side.

"You and Kaspar are two of a kind, and I know you well, for I was once as you are. Troublemakers. I knew it from the beginning," Old Sly said.

"Why is it troublemaking to want to go home?" Josh asked.

"Because *this* is your home now!" Pardo answered earnestly. "*This* is where you will stay. Trying to leave—trying, trying—only makes the others restless; brings discontent. This is our homeland, Canara. So why do we want to be where we can't? Now you must stand trial, and it's all so unnecessary."

With Old Sly rowing, the boat moved across the dark water, and because Josh found the men willing to talk, he asked more: "What is it about you, Pardo, and Leone and Isobel, that you can come and go as you please, to The Edge and back? Some magic potion? 'Sang and something else?"

"'Sang is our tonic, but it's no magic potion. As to why some of us can go to The Edge, I have no answer, except that Isobel and I are as fixed in this place as the roots of a tree. Leone . . . ? I don't know. She seems able to wander about The Edge at will, yet she is as tied to Isobel as a lamb to its ewe. We can go to The Edge, it is true, but we can't go beyond," Pardo replied.

Old Sly nodded. "I've long wondered about this myself. Leone is my daughter, yet she, who prefers Canara, can go anytime to The Edge, while I, who would leave in an instant—yes, leave even her behind and go—am doomed to see no one outside our village."

"Then you are even more foolish than Josh," Pardo snapped. "Here we have everything we never had before. We are protected from those who would persecute us. Here we have peace and respect, yet you would go, if you could, and start things all over again."

The two men grew silent, each alone with his thoughts, until Josh asked finally, "Where was Leone going the night she found me? What was she doing in The Edge?"

"Perhaps Isobel sent her," Pardo replied. "She might have sensed you were out there, and sent Leone to bring you in. You could have stumbled off and never known Canara, or possibly you would have wandered in anyway, but it's good we found you when we did."

"Is it?" Josh asked ruefully, but neither man took it upon himself to answer.

It wasn't until the rowboat drew close to

land that Josh noticed the villagers from Canara waiting on the bank. Lanterns illuminated their faces, and the sobriety of their features gave him reason to suspect, for the first time, that he was in serious trouble.

"Do they always come to the bridge when the dogs bark?" he asked.

"The way they barked tonight—the whole village knew something was amiss," said Pardo.

"Can't I just work extra to pay for another boat?" Josh asked. "Couldn't you take all my wages for digging and order a new boat from the traders the next time they come?"

"Your wages would scarcely pay for an oar," Old Sly scoffed.

"It's more than the boat, lad, it's the law," Pardo told him. "Having only one boat threatens the lives of us all. If one of the boats is out, then the other must be at the ready in case there is an accident—should a child fall in, for example. You did not ask, you took. And having borrowed the boat, you took no care to tie it up. Everyone must have his say."

"But I didn't mean to hurt or rob you. That wasn't it at all."

"An example must be made," said Old Sly as they disembarked under the watchful eyes of the crowd. Josh saw Mavis and Gil standing to one side and felt shame.

It was a silent procession back to the village

clearing, and Josh was surprised that everyone seemed to have turned out, late though it was—young children as well as the old. *Like a public hanging,* he thought dryly. *Where are the picnic baskets? Might as well make a night of it.* He wondered what would have happened to him if he had taken *both* boats.

Lanterns hung here and there to dispel the darkness, but it was not a festive gathering as it had been at The Stop. The elderly sat on benches brought out from the cookhouse to take advantage of the evening air, but the rest stood about in small groups, whispering. Children watched solemnly.

Pardo motioned Josh to a bench up front, facing the others.

"He is accused," he said simply, pointing to Josh, and sat down.

Old Sly stood up then and told how the boat had been taken without permission, and how Josh had not even taken pains to tie it up, and now the boat was lost. A murmur ran through the crowd.

"Hang him," someone said.

Josh started. He could not believe this.

"Yes, stone him!" called someone else.

"No!" cried Mavis.

"It's a boat, boys, not a life," Pardo reminded them.

"It *could* have been a life," said a woman, a small boy on her lap.

And another added, "It was a low thing to do, so make it the lowliest of penalties. Fill one of the privy pits and dig us another."

"Aye!" cried the woman holding the boy.

Then a loud giggle from the girl named Helena. "He won't be fit to be with! Even his hair will stink!"

"He'll be humbled," agreed Eulaylia, nodding.

"Is it a vote then?" asked Pardo.

"Aye."

fourteen

THE defendant was never given a chance to say a word, but Josh had nothing to say. What good would it do? If they got him started, he would tell them that like frogs in hot water, sitting passively as the temperature rose until they were boiled to death, the people of Canara were wasting their lives accepting the unacceptable. Why didn't they rail against the power that held them here? he wanted to ask. Why didn't they band together and seek out the source?

Old Sly stood guard over Josh in the stable that night, but it was wholly unnecessary. Where would he go? In the morning, on their rest day, while the others ambled about, Pardo took Josh to the oldest of the privies. The roof of the shelter had been removed, as well as the privacy fence and the toilet bench, and from the pit below, the stench of human waste was so foul and strong that Josh gagged to be near it.

"Every few years, we fill in the old ones and dig new," Pardo said, handing Josh a shovel. He pointed to a space some five feet away. "Dig a new here, and with each shovelful, fill the old."

Josh burned with humiliation. A small group of villagers gathered to watch. Children ran over to cover their mouths and noses with their hands, making exaggerated gagging noises, then scampered on, jeering at him in their play. There was nothing for Josh to do but dig. He took off his shirt, laid it on the grass, and then—bare-chested, except for the grimy tape around his rib cage—took the shovel and began.

When he started out, his muscles rested, he found he could lift a shovelful of dirt and, turning his entire body so that it would not twist his torso, toss the dirt into the open pit all in one swift movement. But it was not long before the turning hurt his back, and the rib, which was close to healed, began to complain inside his chest. His palms blistered, and Pardo came by to tape them up. Spectators moved on as more came to take their place.

It was necessary finally to walk each shovelful over to the stinking hole, to face the thick dark waste below, and each time his throat tightened, his stomach rebelled, and Josh held his breath until he could turn away.

His head began to throb. Lord, what he'd

give to be gone. Every glance down into the feces was a look at the worst of humankind and yet, he reminded himself, his own waste was present, no less offensive than the rest. *This is what I've become,* he thought.

After a while the stink seemed to cling to his skin, his clothes. He worked faster and faster to cover the foul surface of the old pit, and when that was done, the job seemed easier. With each shovelful the new pit grew deeper, the old more shallow, until finally, many hours later, he had filled the old pit and sat in the shade with a cup of water before he began the cleaning of the toilet bench. It had to be repositioned over the new hole, the privacy fence and roof reinstalled. His weary limbs begged for a reprieve.

The gawking onlookers had disappeared now and only Gil came by, practicing his running. "Look at me, Josh! I'm flying!" he called gleefully, grinning broadly, and then called over his shoulder, "Stinking job, huh?"

Josh stopped working momentarily, glad for the respite, and studied the round-bodied boy, who was practicing, he could tell, to keep his pace steady.

"Did you do your warm-ups?" he called. "*All* of them—the back stretch? The Achilles stretch?"

Gil slowed and finally trotted over to Josh. "Yes, but the back roll is still hard for me."

Running in place, he patted his abdomen. "Too much belly."

"You'll lose it," Josh said, smiling. "I can tell already. But don't forget to jog between runs. You're working on stamina, remember, not just speed."

He watched the boy take off again. How little it took to make him happy. Just a little attention. Daniel and Eulaylia were older parents than most, and Josh could imagine they did not have the time to give Gil all he needed. What Josh could show this kid if they ever left Canara! How he could open his eyes!

As he worked at digging a post hole, an idea crossed his mind he had not thought of before. If what Old Sly said was true, that a boat could drift downriver but he and the others could not, perhaps a bottle could get through to the outside, a bottle with a message in it—that old standby. Perhaps the solution to his rescue was far simpler than he had suspected.

It was something to think about while he finished his task, yet the cleaning of the toilet bench was even more repulsive than the digging, for the spots and stains of human bodies ringed each of the two holes, crusted the openings, and finally, unable to hold back any longer, Josh put his head between his knees and threw up. Then, looking down into his own vomit, he heaved again.

He bathed in the river when his ordeal was over, and skipped the evening meal, wording and rewording the message in his mind:

A VILLAGE HELD HOSTAGE SOMEWHERE IN THE APPALACHIANS, POSSIBLY TEN-NESSEE, A PLACE CALLED CANARA.

And then, to insure that would-be rescuers came, he added:

ABUNDANT GINSENG.

And finished with:

COME AT ONCE. JOSHUA VARDY, C/O CAROL

MCGRATH, DALLAS, TEXAS.

Second task: to find a bottle with a tight-fitting cap.

Back in the stable, he closed his eyes as night rolled in, wishing for sleep for his aching limbs, too tense to let it come. He hoped he had not done his rib any serious damage. But, strangely, it was not his body that troubled him, but his thoughts.

The straw crumpled softly as someone moved toward him. Josh opened his eyes. Mavis lay down on her side a few feet away, head resting on her hand.

"Hello," she said.

He turned in the other direction and placed one arm across his forehead. "Visiting hours? Come to see the prisoner?"

"Don't joke, Josh."

"I'm not."

"I'm all mixed up inside," she told him.

"Welcome to the club."

"What?"

"Just an expression. I'm mixed up, too."

"I was angry at you for losing my grandfather's boat. It takes a long time to build another, you know. Leone and Pardo only see the traders twice in four seasons, so it will be some time before we get the oarlocks."

Josh rolled over to face her. "I borrowed it. I hadn't meant to lose or steal it, and I'm really sorry it got away."

"I was angry that you would risk so much by going over there. It's the same as if someone broke into your bank. Kaspar told me about banks."

"I didn't even know what was over there! I just knew it must be something awfully important or they wouldn't have guard dogs at the entrance. I thought I could leave Canara."

"That's the part that scares me. That you would do something so dangerous to get out, to go back. What is it you have Beyond that we don't have here—that makes you so desperate to leave?"

It was the question Josh had been wrestling with himself. "I'm not sure." He didn't know why he put out his hand just then and stroked the back of hers, lying limply there on the straw.

Mavis, the Amazon girl, looked smaller here in the shadow of the haymow, younger than she seemed in daylight, her voice more timid.

"I asked Eulaylia once why it was I couldn't leave—if I wanted to, that is—and she said it was because I am different. All of us in Canara are different," Mavis ventured.

"You've been brainwashed, that's all," Josh said. He put out one arm, inviting her to curl up next to him for comfort, and she wrapped her own around him. "Melungeons have been told they are 'different' for so long you're beginning to believe it." He liked the warmth of her against him, the scent of her skin.

"No, the Melungeons of Canara, I mean," she explained. "We *are* different. Because of the way we live here. And because of . . . of the Changeover."

"The what?" he murmured.

"They say . . . Pardo has told us . . . that those with pure Melungeon blood—direct descendants of the Santa Elena settlers—have the ability to live forever if they reach a certain age. Then they become young again, and all the events of their present existence are added to those of the past. They are the 'Old Who Remember.'"

"Mavis, that's nonsense."

"Is it? Is there any place in Beyond that is like Canara, where to go forward you must first go back?"

"No, but if some of you live forever, it means you are a kind of ghost, and you certainly feel like flesh and blood to me." When she didn't reply, he asked, "So who are the purebreds in Canara? Who will live forever?"

"I didn't say they *would*, Josh. I said if they don't die before the Changeover, they begin again, just as they have been doing for a long, long time. I'm not sure who they are. Perhaps they don't even know themselves until it happens."

"Isobel?"

"I think so. She certainly seems to be getting to that age, and if she does—if she doesn't meet up with an accident or illness before then—well, it's this that keeps Canara going. Pardo says we need people who know the past in order to preserve our future."

"What about the rest of you?"

"I've heard that there can be an immortal in every generation, and sometimes we joke about it—we who are young. We kid about which of us it might be. But it's not a joke, Josh. It's real. At least, I've been told that it's so."

He could not believe she swallowed all this. "And if, for some reason, something happened to the 'Old Who Remember'—before they got to the Changeover—then Canara would mix with the rest of the world and you could go anywhere you wanted?"

"Should that happen, Eulaylia says, there is a good chance Canara would cease to exist at all, and we along with it."

"Sounds pretty hypothetical," Josh said. "Did you ever think, though, that none of this applies to you? How many others in the village were born of one parent from inside Canara and one from Beyond? Melungeon or not, that makes you a half-breed, right?"

"I know. I've thought of it, too. And that's why my grandfather dislikes you so. If I ever took it in my head to leave, who knows what might happen."

Josh sighed. "How will you ever know unless you try? But why torture yourself, Mavis? You can't leave, I can't leave. Nobody knows how."

"I know all that, but I can't stop thinking," she said.

"Neither can I. I don't even know why I'm so eager for you to see the world through my eyes. Who am I to decide what will make someone else happy?"

For a long time they lay in the shadows, Josh stroking her hair. He was thinking how he would have felt if he'd ever lain this way with Karen Shroeder. Oh, man! It wasn't that he didn't feel anything with Mavis—he did, and hoped she didn't notice—just that there was a lot more to think about here than that.

Finally, when she had gone, a dark figure slid down from the top of the haymow and, in a cloud of dust, Kaspar landed on the floor beside Josh.

"The privy stink can't be too bad," he said. "She sure got close enough."

Josh bolted upright. "What do you want?"

"She knows a way out, doesn't she?"

"If she does, she didn't tell me, and if she does she hasn't used it. Go figure."

"She tell you about the equinox?"

Josh's heart sank. It was his last hope—the schoolhouse. Kaspar had thought of it, too? "She told me they go to school on that day."

Kaspar sat tapping his boot with the edge of his knife, nodding in time to the rhythm. "They all go school that evening to sing. Tradition. All but the old and sick. I'm making a plan, and you're—" He stopped as he heard Old Sly arriving with a bucket of feed. "We'll talk later," he said, and, climbing up the hay to the small window above, wedged himself through and dropped to the ground on the other side.

fifteen

THE question haunted Josh in the days to come—should he try the message in the bottle or the schoolhouse or both? But as the time drew closer, the question seemed to answer itself, for no bottle was to be found with a cap tight enough to use. The plastic aspirin bottle in Josh's pack was too small to be worthy of anyone's attention, the cap unsure.

Was he disappointed or not? The only acceptable answer was yes, of course, and yet, Josh was beginning to detect a flicker of doubt. If he stayed in Canara, he would never have to face a new, uncertain life in Dallas. He would never have to risk being lowest man on the totem pole—possibly not making a team at all, any of them. He fought against this fear, banishing it from his mind, ever watchful it would creep back in again.

That the schoolhouse would appear on the

equinox was, according to Mavis, as sure as autumn itself—sure as autumn in Canara, that is, for here the seasons were shorter, the solstices closer together, time of a different sort than Josh had known back in Massachusetts. He noticed that Gil had been right—the hills that he had seen straight ahead as he came out of the stable each morning, hills that lay in overlapping waves, had slowly migrated to the west, to be replaced by knobbier-looking vistas; and then, these, too, had moved off center stage and the undulating hills were back again. Josh just accepted that it was so.

He began to prepare himself mentally for the leave-taking—to give no outward sign that he was going, so that Kaspar would not guess and come along. Yet he found he was worrying about Mavis and what would happen to her. Thinking about Gil, too. There were even times his thoughts drifted to old Isobel, aging and alone in her cottage when Leone was out with the horse and wagon.

These would not hold him here, however. Fair was fair. He had not asked to come to Canara and would feel no guilt upon leaving. Well, some perhaps. But there were problems wherever you went. Aunt Carol down in Texas had her share, and so had he. Still, he looked at Mavis, curious but hesitant about the world outside, and imagined going to high school with her—imagined her trying out for the girls' soccer team. Gad! What a player she'd make! Imagined her singing in a choral group. Wouldn't she love it, though?

And young Gil, who hardly even knew that Beyond was there—who accepted that Canara was to be his future. Where was the guarantee, however, that Beyond would make them any happier, a place where a traffic accident could change your life as surely as a child falling into a river or a cookhouse burning to the ground?

Waiting for the coming equinox, Josh found himself more reflective, calmer, kinder, as though a wound inside himself were healing. He went out each day with the diggers, looking for the elusive ginseng, knowing all the while that there was the largest batch in the world growing on the high rocky island in the river. He assisted Leone with the water barrel at noon when she brought lunch to the diggers, helped Old Sly harness up the horses, and, to all appearances, seemed to be "settling in."

Kaspar noticed.

"You caving in or are you with me?"

"Is this an either-or question?" Josh quipped.

"You didn't tell me when you took Old Sly's boat. You found what was on the island, didn't you? I wormed that out of Gil the first week I was here. Listen, whatever you've thought of doing, I've already tried. You could save yourself a lot of trouble by going in with me. I've got a plan."

"What is it?"

"It's not time yet. I'll let you know. But first you've got to tell me—are you in with me or not?"

"Sure," Josh lied. By the time he was "in" with Kaspar, he'd be out of Canara. He had to stay away from Kaspar, have as little to do with him as possible.

"It's the old crone," Kaspar said before he left. "Keep your eye on her."

Josh tried to do so, not out of suspicion but out of concern. Keeping an eye on Isobel, however, was difficult to do, because no one ever saw more than her head or hand at the window. When Leone pushed her through the village on their evening outing, no one saw more than a blanketed bundle in the bottom of the cart. There were times Josh wondered if the woman was still alive, and whether mad, mute Leone might be wheeling around a corpse. But now and then he would hear a faint wail from the bundle, and Leone would gently reach down to adjust the blanket.

To show his willingness to fit into the community and provoke no questions, Josh went with Gil and some of the other young men one day to castrate a large boar that was getting mean and threatening the children. Unable to sire offspring anymore once the deed was done, the animal would be allowed to grow fat, Old Sly explained, and then they would roast him on a holiday. Three of the dogs Josh had seen at the bridge were brought in for the hunt, and once again, the older folk smiled at the young men as they set off to find the boar. Another rite of passage, Josh decided; work both ritual and necessary.

The dogs were eager for the chase, and there was a wild scramble through the woods— over rocks and undergrowth so thick they thought they had lost the beast. Then his wild snort came again as he shook a dog loose and went charging once more.

Gil was clearly excited as he clambered after the animal, splitting the air with his raucous calls and bellows. He was trapped momentarily on a stump when the boar turned suddenly and charged, but a dog intervened, changing the wild hog's course, and Gil escaped without injury, shouting all the louder.

Chad Tolliver was the one who cornered the beast at last. One of the dogs had the animal by a foreleg, another by the ear, the third by the tail, and once the boar was on the ground, they held him there while Chad approached with his hunting knife. A flash of steel, a bellow and jolt of the pig, the smell of blood and excrement, the puddle of red beneath the animal's leg, the wound, and then Chad called off the dogs. The boar, wild with pain and fury, made a pass at the nearest man, then ran blindly in circles a moment or two before heading, bellowing still, up a rocky path and into the trees.

"Got 'im!" Chad sang out, holding up a gray lump in his hand, and Josh's stomach lurched.

Mavis spoke to Josh that evening at the well.

"You went out after the boar today, I know," she said. "Pardo was pleased, but my grandfather calls you a *converso*."

"What's that?"

She smiled ruefully. "It is an old, old word from our history, the name given to Melungeon Jews and Muslims who were forced to convert to Christianity, for not all of them fled the Inquisition. No one quite believed them, and with good reason. Who truly believes out of fear? Old Sly doesn't know whether you are sincere or not."

"It's like you said, Mavis: I can either get along, or I can be miserable. I don't choose to be miserable."

"But deep down, I wonder if you're happy here."

"Deep down, I wonder about *you*."

She gave no answer to that. "Soon it will be the equinox," she told him, "and for that one day Eulaylia will hold classes in the schoolhouse. It's like a holiday. When instruction is over, we push the desks to one side and sing and dance. We take every occasion to dance."

"That's good. Celebrate while you can," said Josh.

"While we can? Why not always?"

"Of course, always! Why not?" Josh corrected himself. She was right.

In the days that followed, planning his escape, Josh wondered if he should write a note of some sort, so that if this didn't work out there would be some record of his intentions, a kind of closure to his passing. Perhaps on equinox night when they were dancing, he could slip it in the pocket of Mavis's skirt. When she found it, he felt sure she would keep it.

The morning of the equinox, Josh followed the others along the path that led to the schoolhouse. He had explored it once, he remembered, and found nothing, but he was used to surprises by now.

"The equinox and the solstices, they all seem to be special occasions here in Canara," he remarked to Gil.

"And the nights of the full moon—don't forget those," said Gil. "We'll have fun together, won't we, Josh?"

In answer, Josh asked, "Will I see anything particular on the winter solstice?" as though he were looking forward already to his first year in Canara.

"There's a church at the winter solstice. We sing. Then the old folks go home and we dance. We always dance. At the spring equinox there's a store, but it has nothing in it now. We've taken all the tins of food we found; nothing else is useful. But we have a party anyway."

"And the summer solstice?" Josh asked.

"Ah, in the summer it is a house—a huge house that someone lived in once. We take a banquet with us and go through all the rooms, sit in all the chairs. We go up and down the grand staircase, as though we all lived in Beyond. A fine time it is, too."

I will not be around to see your grand house, Josh thought.

The school loomed before them, as solid a structure as Josh had ever seen, sitting on ground he knew he had traversed that was mere mud and leaves before.

Eulaylia was at the desk in front when they went inside, along with Pardo and Daniel. They welcomed the students and everyone sat, smaller children at the front, young men and women at the back.

"It was the best of times, it was the worst of times," Eulaylia began, reading from Dickens, and while she read, Josh's eyes scanned the doors and windows to see how he would get back inside the schoolhouse once it was closed for the night.

After Eulaylia's reading and the spelling bee, during which those who had misspelled a word were eliminated from the competition with great merriment and shouting, Pardo gave the history lesson. It was one Josh had never learned in school, but he had no doubt it was authentic.

Pardo's lined face was the color of sunlit copper, his eyes the deepest blue. His voice rose and fell in pitch, as though this tale had been told many times before.

"On the last day of July," he said, looking somewhere above and beyond the heads of his listeners, "the year 1502, off the island of Jamaica, Columbus came upon a strange people on a ship not familiar to those waters. It was forty feet long and eight feet in diameter, with a shaded pavilion in the center, much like a Mayan Indian design. But to Columbus, it looked like the Moorish galleys he had often seen in the Mediterranean Sea. There were some forty men and women on this galley, and unlike the Jamaican Indians, these people wore clothing: sleeveless shirts with bright colors and designs like those Columbus had seen in Granada, so he has written.

"The people carried a cargo of tools—copper, and forges for working the copper," Pardo continued. "But perhaps what interested him most was that the women aboard this ship covered their faces, like the women of Granada. These were not Mayan Indians, I tell you, but Muslims who had reached the New World before Columbus. Even he, my students, considered the possibility. If the historians will not tell the truth, we shall, for we in Canara are making our own history in our new homeland."

How? thought Josh. *Who will find you or even know about you if you can't ever leave this place?* Were they trapped because of their own design, he wondered, or by forces beyond their control? Did they even know? And how could he help them? By leaving and telling everyone what he had seen and heard? By leaving and telling no one? By not leaving at all? Tonight was his last chance to go, perhaps, for the next few months. His *only* chance, maybe. Should he leave? Stay?

He was going.

Old Daniel talked next of moon and stars, of math and measurements, time and space. And finally, when younger heads had dropped to desktops and older minds had begun to wander, class was adjourned and school dismissed until the evening's singing and dancing began.

Josh had never felt so torn. He clearly did not want to spend the rest of his life—the rest of the year, even—in Canara, but in some ways it was as though he belonged. As though the world of sports and proms, applause and write-ups, was only one part of him, and the rest—the soul, perhaps—was made for here. Was it really this that kept him back, however, or a lack of courage to begin again? To begin in a new place where no one knew what he could do, who he was, what he had done?

As the students walked back to the village to prepare for the evening's festivities, Mavis clutched Josh's arm tightly, as if guessing somehow that he was going to leave.

"Dance with me tonight," she pleaded. "My feet want to fly, I'm so restless."

He joked, "I'll wear out long before you. You'll have to hold me up." And then he inquired, "How long can we stay? If we feel like dancing all night, can we?"

"Not all night, surely."

"Why not?"

"The equinox. It wouldn't do. I mean, the schoolhouse wouldn't *be*."

How accepting she was of things. Where were the whys? He wanted to ask what would happen if the villagers *didn't* go home, but was afraid she would guess his plan, and so he kept it to himself.

As they had the night they went to The Stop, the young people bathed first before dinner. Josh unwrapped and discarded the dirty tape that had bound his chest, and was glad he had thought to rinse out and dry his cotton shirt—the armpits had become unbearable. Back in the stable he was just leaning over to tie his sneakers when his head was suddenly jerked backward by a hand gripping his hair and he felt the sharp blade of a knife against his windpipe.

"With me or against me?" Kaspar said through clenched teeth, giving another jerk to Josh's hair.

In terror, Josh's lips refused to reply.

Another shake of his hair, and the knife grazed the skin of his Adam's apple. "With me or against me?" Kaspar repeated.

"W-with," said Josh, eyes wild, but not as wild as Kaspar's.

"Tonight, then." Kaspar released his hold on Josh, but the point of the knife remained on his throat. "It's the crone and her power that keep us here. Take her out, and we're free. Tonight, when everyone's gathered at the schoolhouse, we leave during the last dance and we slit their throats—Isobel's and Leone's. I'll do Leone, you take the old woman. It's a female thing—the spell, the witchcraft. When the dance is over, everyone will come back to find them strung up like geese on a line by the cookhouse, and the spell will be broken. We'll sell off the ginseng over on the island, and you and I will go home rich. You fail, and I'll cut you to ribbons. I'll hang you up like dried cod."

Something clunked at Josh's feet, and he

saw that Kaspar had tossed him a butcher knife.

But once again Kaspar grabbed his hair, and again Kaspar's knife pressed so hard against Josh's throat that he felt a small trickle of blood run down his neck.

"Who are you with?" Kaspar questioned.

"Y-you."

"Who do you kill?"

"Isobel."

"And what will we be when it's over?"

"Free."

sixteen

FOOD sat in Josh's mouth at supper, but wouldn't go down.

"What happened to your throat?" Mavis asked him, running her finger lightly over his neck.

Josh forced himself to swallow. "Got in a scrape with Kaspar. Nothing serious."

"Stay away from him, Josh. He's evil. What was it about?"

"Kaspar and I are always arguing about something," he said in answer.

The young men and women came to the table in freshly washed clothes. Their elders looked on approvingly, and the younger children, who would undoubtedly fall asleep before the evening was over, jumped and wrestled and teased, knowing only that this evening was special somehow, and, like children everywhere, glad for any diversion.

The knife Kaspar had given Josh was now tucked inside his belt, and if he moved the wrong way, or tried to bend to one side, the tip dug into his thigh. When the crowd set out finally for the schoolhouse again, Josh found himself walking stiffly because of the knife, and Mavis was quick to notice.

"Your rib again?"

He nodded. "I hurt it fighting with Kaspar."

"It will never heal properly if you keep jostling it," she scolded. "I've never known anyone to win in a fight with Kaspar. No one."

"Some fights you don't win," he told her.

They walked a half mile—back through an orchard, then a wood, lanterns swinging as they had when they went to The Stop. This time many of the village elders followed, for the night at the schoolhouse was a bit less wild and more restrained than the nights at The Stop, Josh gathered. Leone and Isobel, however, were not among them, Isobel being too feeble.

It could have been Christmas Eve for all the joy and anticipation, Josh mused, but not for him. Chad Tolliver, he noticed, was teasing Mavis, and had made a crown of autumn leaves for her head. She flushed and wore it gaily, and Chad looked pleased.

The singing came first, old folk songs Josh didn't know—"Song to the Moon" and "Emilia." But when livelier tunes were introduced, the old voices gave way to young, and then the dancing began with Sylvania and her new husband first on the floor.

Josh was startled, but not surprised, to find that his shirt was soaked with perspiration.

"Are you ill?" Mavis questioned as they whirled about the floor together, boots making thumping noises on the boards. But Josh knew it was not sickness, nor the note he had slipped in her pocket. It was, instead, a moment of recognition—that in Canara's history, he saw his own. Going backward in time, he saw the future. He had once lived in a place where he knew who he was, where there was laughter and home, family and friends, and now he would start all over again among strangers. Fate had dealt him a blow that would change his life forever, but it would still be a life, and the future was up to him. He was still the person he had always been. That had not changed.

It wasn't this that caused him to grab Mavis by the waist and whirl her faster and faster toward the door, but it was a conviction that the person he was needed to do what he was about to do.

"Josh!" she cried, laughing.

He whirled her still, down the path and toward the trees.

"Josh?" she said again. "It's a night for dancing, but not out here."

"It's a night for murder," he breathed, stopping suddenly behind a tree, his chest heaving.

She tensed, and pulled away.

"Mavis, listen . . ." Josh released her and struggled to get his breath. Then he told her of Kaspar's plot.

She stared incredulously. "He wouldn't!"

"He would, Mavis." He pointed to his own throat.

"Then tell the men! Raise the alarm!"

"First help me get the women to safety. Old Sly may not believe me. I was the one who took the boat, after all, and Kaspar will deny everything."

"Kaspar!" Mavis kept saying as they broke into a run. "I would suspect him of many things, but hardly that. Surely he's mad."

They reached the stable breathless, then took the back path to Isobel's hut and pounded on the door.

Leone came to the door with a lantern, her hair down, and looked at them quizzically.

"Mother," said Mavis. "You must come with us, you and Isobel. Kaspar plans to kill you."

Leone's face contorted in disbelief, and she placed her hand questioningly on her chest.

"Yes, you and Isobel," Josh repeated. "We'll take you to Eulaylia's and ring the alarm."

They looked around for Isobel and saw the small blanketed heap on the bed. As Josh picked her up, she gave a faint cry, like that of a young bird, and when he tucked the covers back from around her face, he found—amid the wisps of fallen white hair—a face not unlike that of a newborn babe. A small clawlike hand reached out, and Isobel clasped his thumb, pulling it to the ancient lips of her infant self.

Josh gasped, speechless. He sensed that somehow she had crossed over, and was beginning again. That as long as she lived on, so would Canara. He stared wonderingly at Isobel, then at Mavis, who stood with one hand covering her mouth.

As they started back through the darkness, Josh carrying Isobel, the wind picked up, and Mavis's skirt whipped and snapped like a sail flapping on a boat.

"The equinoctial gale," Mavis said knowingly. "Pardo has explained it to us."

It was another part of his education that was deficient, Josh observed; however, it was not the tempest outside that consumed him, but the turmoil within. It was quite possible that Kaspar was right—that Isobel herself was the key to their coming and going, and that only in her death and the deaths of the Old Who Remember would the spell be broken. Even so, he carried the shriveled body as carefully as he would have the newborn child she was coming to be, and when they reached Eulaylia's empty cottage, laid her gently upon the bed. Leone helped prop the old woman up on pillows, adjusted the swaddling blanket. From somewhere in the darkness of the breathing hole, Josh knew that her two old eyes were watching.

"It is the night," came the cracked voice, only a whisper now. "The Changeover. The equinox. Day equals night, and night equals day, and it is the same the world over."

Josh wondered, his heart beginning to race. "Is this night special for me, Isobel?"

"When you lose your fear, Joshua," the high voice came again, "you will be able to see the way out." And then, so softly only he could hear it, "Go."

To go forward, you must go back, she had told him once. To what? To the security of who he was as a young boy, he suddenly realized— safe in the love of his family, his heritage. Before there were doubts, before there were disappointments, to the time one looks about and feels he can do anything at all. To a sense of his own inner worth. It was this he needed to see him through.

Josh felt charged with energy, hope rushing through his body like blood. He could only conclude that life renewed itself here in Canara, again and again, that each generation went back to the distant source. A spell unbroken, a village undisturbed, a homeland at last. Its secret was safe with him. Somehow Isobel had seen that he, too, had touched that source, and had given him her blessing.

As Mavis and Leone waited, he went to the door and listened. Now and then, carried along on the wind, came the sound of distant music, the thump of pounding feet, before the shriek of the gale covered all.

"Lock the door," he said to Mavis as he prepared to leave. "Bolt it securely."

But Mavis refused to stay. Once outside, when the door clicked after them, she grabbed his arm and studied his face. Did she guess?

He was twisted suddenly from her grasp, and instantly Josh knew that Kaspar had come. Before he reached for the butcher knife tucked in the waistband of his jeans, he instinctively reached for Kaspar's, and cut his hand on the cold steel, which was pointed at his neck.

Mavis screamed and ran toward the clearing, but Josh was locked in combat with a man half crazed, who had lost his moral compass and replaced it with a knife. Wrestling Kaspar to the ground, Josh managed to free the weapon from his grasp, tossing both that and his own as far as he could fling them.

Clang! Clang! Mavis was ringing the bell by the cookhouse, and she rang it again and again, two by two, the sound of alarm. *Clang! Clang!* . . . *Clang! Clang!* it pealed out over Canara.

Hand against hand, Josh pressed Kaspar's wrist to the ground. But Kaspar struggled free and wrapped his hands around Josh's throat until he struggled to breathe. Over and over they tumbled, while the earth throbbed with the sound of running feet. And then Old Sly and Daniel were pulling them apart, other hands pushed forward to help, and Mavis came running as more people gathered.

"He is accused!" she cried, pointing at Kaspar. "He would kill us—Leone and Isobel. Josh, too."

Kaspar's knife lay there on the ground, and Old Sly picked it up.

"Who is witness?" Pardo asked, arriving breathless.

"I am," Mavis answered.

"And where is Isobel?"

"Safe in Eulaylia's house."

The crowd that had been dancing only a short time before was gathering now for a trial inside the cookhouse. The wind blew stronger still, and as the door closed behind them and Kaspar was hustled to the front of the room, a string of curses poured from his lips.

When all had gathered, Josh had no choice but to recount the treachery Kaspar had proposed—how he had planned to slit the throats of the two women. Josh could see the outcome of the trial as clearly as if it had been written there on the wall—the accusations, the voices arguing back and forth over what should be done, the sky beginning to change . . .

The time! But what time was it? Josh didn't know, only that the evening had seemed young when he had danced Mavis out of the school-house, and now it was not. He glanced across the clearing at her and saw her reading his note.

"Stone him!" he heard the cry go up.

He could not stop this, he knew. *Go!* he told himself. There is nothing here for you. *Go!* Isobel had whispered.

Josh edged back through the crowd until he reached the door, then ran to the stable and picked up his bag. He would not be missed. Mavis had his note as well as his good-bye. Isobel and Leone were safe.

He checked once more to be sure he had everything—money belt, airline ticket, the little silver he had earned digging ginseng—and then, pack slung over one shoulder, he headed for the path to the schoolhouse, giving wide berth to the clearing so he would not have to witness the execution.

But he heard no cries from that direction now. The wind had picked up even stronger so that he leaned into its force, but along with the wind he heard a sound almost like marching— like many footsteps, all heading in the same direction, and when he came to the place where

the path branched off from the clearing, he was
dismayed to see, in the light of the lanterns, the
villagers returning once again to the schoolhouse.

seventeen

HE stared, dumbstruck, then silently fell in beside them. How could he leave with everyone there? Had Isobel got his hopes up for nothing?

As he moved past the older folk at the end of the procession and neared the front of the line, he saw that Kaspar, fast in the grip of a few husky men, was being led to the very door of the schoolhouse.

No! The sentence was deportation, then? Kaspar himself looked puzzled.

Josh dropped his pack and stood on the edge of the crowd, watching, bewildered, as Kaspar was marched up the steps, shoved inside, and the door locked after him. Josh was the one to whom Isobel and Leone owed their lives, yet it was Kaspar who got to leave?

Something was amiss, however. From inside the small building, Kaspar suddenly began to beat against the walls. The schoolhouse was fading, as though caught in a light fog. First the roof began to disappear from view, then the rafter window, then the top of the door frame, and finally, where the building had once stood, there was nothing at all.

Josh exhaled and turned blindly away. It could have been him! *He* could have been on his way to Texas now! When he looked again, people were leaving, going back down the path to the village, murmuring gravely among themselves. Pardo, however, stood nearby.

"It was justice," the man said. "It had to be done."

Josh stared. "It's *not* the way out, then?"

"No, lad. Not that."

"What will happen to him?"

Pardo shrugged. "That's not for us to know. Another equinox, when the schoolhouse comes again, we will see."

"You all knew Kaspar hated it here," Josh said. "You knew he couldn't be trusted. Why did you wait until he'd tried something like this?"

"You still don't understand," Pardo told him. "We have no power to release or to keep you. However much we wished to be rid of Kaspar, it was he who made his own prison."

Josh stood transfixed, his eyes on the place the schoolhouse had stood. "If I had been inside just now . . ."

"That would have been unwise," Pardo answered.

"How do you know he won't get out and come back here again?"

"Because once, long ago, another left with the schoolhouse. And when the autumnal equinox was on us again, we opened the door to the building and out fell a heap of bones." Pardo raised his lantern to see the path in front of him and began to maneuver himself over the rocky ground. But Josh stopped him.

"Pardo, please! I have to know. If Kaspar made his own prison, what about the rest of you? Could you break the spell if you wanted?"

The man's eyes were so deep, yet intent, his face so lined, yet alive, that Josh knew that he, like Isobel, was ageless. "As long as there are the Old Who Remember, we build our own wall, it seems. It's that which holds us in, I believe, and keeps the world at bay. But then . . . is that so bad? To have a homeland at last? I think not." He set out again, turning once and, raising the lantern even higher to see Josh's face, said simply, "Good-bye, Joshua." And went on.

Josh stared after him, then at the darkness of the woods.

"Go," he said aloud to himself.

He startled. "What?" he asked the darkness.

And again, as though another self had taken command, he said the word "Go!" He had been blown off course and had found himself far from home, but he would make of it a new beginning. Something seemed different now, not in the landscape, but inside himself. A changeover. His legs moved as though powered by some internal engine. He walked forward, across the place the schoolhouse had stood, surprised to see a path, a narrow trail among the brush and brambles. A lemon moon led the way.

He put out his hands to part the bushes.

"Josh!"

Mavis came running up behind him, her cheeks flushed, breath coming in short little gasps.

"I knew you were leaving," she said. "I knew you were going back, and then I found your note in my pocket."

"I'm not going back, I'm going forward."

He saw that she was holding something in her hand, and looked at her wonderingly as she placed a watch in his palm.

"All I could think was that you were leaving without any remembrance of Canara, and so I brought you this. It belonged to my father, I was told, but I have no need of it here."

"Are you sure you want me to have it?"

"Please."

He saw that it was an old watch, the windup kind, and judging the time to be about a quarter past midnight, he set it, then held it to his ear. He heard a faint ticking.

"Mavis . . ." he began in gratitude, and then was even more astonished when she linked her arm in his and began walking along with him.

"Where are you going?"

"With you."

He blinked. "Do you know what you're doing?"

"I feel so strange," she said in answer.

"When did you decide to do this?" he asked, closing his hand over hers.

"Tonight."

"You've said no good-byes?"

"They'll know soon enough. It would be difficult in any case to say good-bye to my grandfather. And Leone . . ." She hesitated. Then, almost breathlessly, "Mother spoke, Josh! She saw I was leaving, and spoke to me!"

"What did she say?"

"Just my name."

"That's hardly a blessing. She'll miss you."

"I know."

"You brought nothing with you!"

"I have silver. I can buy what I need."

Seeing is believing, Josh told himself. At what point would the path loop back upon itself, circling, circling? At what point would they both turn around to see that they had been walking an hour or two and had gone only a few yards from the village?

Mavis walked determinedly, but still she was thoughtful, and so to keep up their spirits, Josh told her about the high school he had come from, about the girls' soccer team, the school newspaper, the chorus. About Aunt Carol and how she'd never had a daughter. He described her home in Texas—the porch, the plants. He said maybe Aunt Carol would let her have the corner bedroom, the one overlooking the pond, and told her about the boys who would call and want to take her out.

But Mavis's footsteps had begun to slow.

"I must go back," she said suddenly.

He looked at her in dismay. "Why?"

"I have a mother. She needs me. Oh, Josh, now that she's said my name . . ."

He nodded, numb with disappointment.

She wavered. "Do you hate me?"

"Of course not. Go back to her, Mavis. There is something important here you will never find outside."

"I'm Melungeon—Canara is my home." Her eyes were moist.

"I know. I'm Melungeon, too. And I'm going on to what I know. It's as familiar to me as Canara is to you."

They each studied the other's face. At last, taking Josh's hands in hers, Mavis said, "I'll miss you."

He noticed the lightness of her fingers. "I'll

miss you too. But if you come, you will miss so much more." He smiled at her and tried to be poetic. "Songbirds belong in Canara."

She gave him a small smile. "Good-bye, then, Josh. May we both be happy."

"Tell Gil I'll miss him, too."

He kissed her, and as he held her one last time, found she was almost weightless in his arms. He stared as she turned then and walked in the opposite direction, her footsteps making no sound at all.

Josh wheeled about and walked rapidly on, his breath coming short, his eyes dazed. He concentrated on keeping his pace steady, counting each step to keep his mind focused, refusing to dwell on what might or might not be.

So much had changed. Everything he was going to tell his new friends in Texas, he knew he would never tell now. His "ace in the hole" was a card he would never play, for fear that ginseng diggers would descend on the hills en masse, searching for the prize. He would go on to Dallas as the person he was meant to be, that he had found himself to be, without needing the story of Canara to pave his way. No one would begin to understand what it meant to Mavis and Gil and Pardo and Leone—no one would believe him, anyway.

As the hours went by, the sky overhead changed from black to a pinkish gray. He had no lantern, so there were no distinguishing land-marks to either elate or discourage him. He had expected a sunrise, for surely it was past dawn by now, yet the sky retained a copper cast and got neither lighter nor darker, as though time itself were standing still. From far, far away, he heard Mavis's voice—the way she sang when-ever she reached the village. Then it faded, and did not come again.

Josh rounded a bend and this time a hum caught his ear, not unlike the thrubbing on women's washboards at the river, or the low rasp of Pardo's saw in the clearing.

He staggered in disappointment and stopped, unable to confirm what he feared. He could not bear to think it. Could not imagine having to admit he had walked all this way—half the night, it seemed—and was back where he'd started.

Before despair overtook him completely, however, he detected a change in tone. The hum he was hearing was more a low buzz. A rumbling sound that could have been anything at all, but was different somehow from Canara.

And as he came over the last rise in the path, where the trees gave way completely to sky, Josh looked down through the rocky pass, through the cliffs of shale, and there, in the val-ley below, were the lights of the interstate.

AFTERWORD

In 1654, English explorers were told by Native Americans about a colony of bearded people in the Appalachians who wore European clothing, lived in cabins, smelted silver, and dropped to their knees to pray many times a day.

Mediterranean-looking people called "Portugals" were found living among the Powhatans and related tribes of eastern Virginia and in the northern portion of the region then called Carolina. In the southern part of Carolina were similar people calling themselves "Turks."

In the 1690s, French explorers reported finding "Christianized Moors" in the Carolina mountains. And by the mid-1700s, large colonies of these copper-skinned, often blue-eyed people were already well-established in the Tennessee and Carolina mountains. In broken Elizabethan English, they referred to themselves as "Portyghee," or the more mysterious term, "Melungeon."

Over the years, as increasing numbers of Scotch-Irish settlers moved in around them, the Melungeons were driven higher and higher into the mountains, their claim of Portuguese heritage increasingly ridiculed. Pushed off their land, denied their rights, often murdered, they adopted English ways and lost their heritage, their culture, their religion, even their names.

Today, around Newman's Ridge in Tennessee, you may see the last of the true Melungeons, if indeed there are any left.